A **LILAH LOVE** NOVEL

AGENT VS ASSASSIN

NEW YORK TIMES BESTSELLING AUTHOR
LISA RENEE JONES WRITING AS

L.R. JONES

BE THE FIRST TO KNOW!

The best way to be informed of all upcoming books, sales, giveaways, television news (there's some coming soon!), and to get a FREE EBOOK, be sure you're signed up for my newsletter list!

SIGN-UP HERE:
HTTP://LISARENEEJONES.COM/NEWSLETTER-SIGN-UP/

DEAR READERS

Hello lovely readers and welcome back to the world of Lilah Love!

If you have not already read through to book eight, *The Ghost* Assassin, please don't read on as I'm going to recap that book to get you geared up to dive into *Agent vs. Assassin*. We left Lilah in a somewhat precarious situation with her once-dead father-in-law. Well...we all thought he was dead. Even his own son, Kane, thought his father had met his maker already. So now, not only are Lilah and Kane battling the Society, Ghost, another assassin who is offing directors in the government, but now they're faced with the devil himself coming back from the ashes.

To Lilah, it's just another inconvenience in her busy schedule. Her main concern is always how Kane will navigate the cartel world when he has tried his very best to keep it at arm's length. A fact his father despises. But this man's presence is nothing more than a distraction from Lilah's current case. A case we have to travel even further back in time to recap on: *The Ghost Assassin* opened up with Lilah responding to Homeland Security's request for her presence. Only for her to find out it's because her boss, Assistant Director Murphy was found dead in his hotel room. There aren't many leads. Only the card for the diner Lilah frequents often for the world-renowned pie, a Nashville phone number, and that's it. Of course, when one of the figureheads of a government agency is taken down, it makes the leaders in Washington just a little nervous. Soon, Lilah is met with the forces of Director Ellis of Homeland Security, and her new *acting* boss, Interim Director Adams of the FBI. Both of whom have a lot to say about the other, but never the full truth, which only serves to piss Lilah off, especially when they're both trying to claim her as theirs. But Lilah is no ones, well, except maybe Kane's, but he would have to be answering her calls and not evading her questions on what he's doing in order for that to be true.

Where there is one body, there is always more. Lilah battens down the hatches of her team. Requesting that Tic Tac come to New York to be within her and Kane's protection, and Andrew, Lucas, and Jack are all present in their own irritating-to-Lilah ways. Back to that other body, another director is found gunned down in the same manner as Murphy in DC. As Lilah is escorted by Adams to the district of the White House, she is waylaid by the other man vying for her attention, Directory Ellis, who has supposedly been given jurisdiction over her by the president. There's nothing much of substance to be found at the crime scene. It's similar to Murphy's, not a lot out of place, and a murder that is seemingly a professional hit job.

Lilah's presence is requested by none other than the President himself. Safe to say Lilah and probably the only politician she would somewhat respect, only because he's the leader of the free world and doesn't seem to cater to either side of the party aisle, have quite the interesting conversation. Even if it is short and concise, though that's just how Lilah likes it. After that, Lilah is headed back to New York, only for her and Jay to come face to face with Ghost, the number one assassin in the world, and the man who has been intrigued by Lilah in a way Kane thinks is obsession. This news of course pisses Kane off, especially when he learns Ghost let her see his face, and drew his weapon on her. Once she is back home, a sketch artist comes to take Lilah's detailed account of Ghost's appearance.

Meanwhile, the only lead they had on the case was the waitress from the diner, and she has moved to Nashville it seems, which connects to the phone number Murphy had written down too. They don't have much else. That is until Director Ellis shows back up and he comes with case files. There was a committee for government contract approvals. The two dead directors were part of that committee as was Ellis, a few other directors, and the current Vice President. The committee was disbanded three years ago, but it ran for six months. In those six months, the committee screwed over their fair share of individuals... And here is where I will leave you with the final scene from *The Ghost Assassin*...

"What's with those three files?" I ask Ellis, tapping the top one.

"I picked out files that connect to the people I think we screwed the most."

"Oh, joy. You were a wonderful group of do-gooders, weren't you? What's the fourth file sitting to the side?"

"The worst of the lot, but the guy is dead. He killed himself."

"You must have fucked him like a champion," I reply. "What made his life not worth living?"

"Clyde Walker and his company held a top-secret government contract for years. Marie Rodriguez wanted to hand it to someone new, who she said brought a fresh perspective."

"A friend," I assume.

"I suspected as much. I actually voted against the change, but the now VP cast the deciding vote."

"I have something," Jack says, and he's really been remarkably not irritating. I'm not sure what to think about that. "The dark web now thinks the assassin is a newcomer."

"Okay, now you're being irritating," I snap. "First it was for sure one of the top five assassins on that list you gave me. Now, it's someone new. This is guessing and it does us no good."

"Open minds breed open ideas," he counters.

"Whatever the fuck that means. I liked 'horror movie' Jack better than 'motivational speaker' Jack. Either you have something solid, or you don't."

"That's the point," he says. "I do. Apparently, some user on the dark web was asking for an assassin willing to hit government targets. There were no takers. I looked back and found the thread. Screen name DoubleM was asking for a taker."

"When?" I ask.

"April of 2020," he supplies.

Ellis grabs a file and hands it to me. "Look for that date."

He snatches up another himself and three files in, we have nothing. I point at file four. "Check that one."

"I told you. Clyde's dead."

"Someone loved him. When you love someone, you kill for them, right?"

"I'm not sure that's how you show love."

"I guess some of us love harder. Check the file."

He snatches it up and scans the contents, going stone still a minute into his review. "He died in April of 2020." He glances at me. "And the company—Blackhawk Security—is a contract military operation."

"Are you fucking serious?" I snap. "How are you director of Homeland Security? Why isn't this on the top of your list?"

"They were technology-based. This wasn't a bunch of guys going out and killing people. And the company shut down. He had no partner. He has a son in the private sector and a daughter in the Army, but she's well decorated and— you know—she's—"

"A woman," I supply. "Now you had to go and make me think you're a dick I can't work for."

Tic Tac clears his throat. "Houston, I think we have a problem. Clyde's daughter is a trained sniper, and the son is a VP at a firearms company. I'm a data guy, but that seems problematic. Maybe they couldn't hire an assassin, so they just decided to do the dirty work themselves?"

"There was a movie like that," Jack says. "Hmmm. I can't remember the name. But I think—"

"Unless that movie helps in some way, Jack," I snap, "we don't care."

Ellis and I look at each other, an unspoken "oh, fuck" between us. "And I would have known that if I hadn't set the damn file aside," Ellis bites out before he eyes Tic Tac. "Where do they live and where are they now? And can you ping their phones for location?"

"I'm working on it," Tic Tac says.

"Pardon me, Director Ellis," Jack says, oh, so politely, "but there was more to Clyde Walker's Blackhawk operation than technology. Per the dark web, he owned a ranch in Maryland where he trained his staff. There's a big thread there talking about him training killers, and speculation about jobs they did for the government."

Killers like Ghost, I think. "How does the dark web know this, and you don't, Director Ellis?"

"I was lied to," he says. "And so was everyone else on the committee, which makes me question Marie's personal interest in the company."

"I can look into that," Tic Tac offers, "but right now, Mark and Elsa's phones are pinging at the Maryland ranch."

Ellis grabs his phone. "I'll get a team out there."

"No," I say. "If Marie had a personal interest in Blackhawk, so might others. We need to get them to talk and to search the place first. And you should stay here. If the siblings are killing off everyone that voted out Blackhawk, you're a target."

Ellis's jaw sets stubbornly. "I assure you, Agent, I can handle myself. You did good work. I'm going to handle it from here." He stands. "These files need to come with me."

I push to my feet. "This is a mistake."

"Then it's my mistake to make. Thank you for the hard work. I'll contact you after the raid."

When someone does something stupid and they outrank you, plus carry a gun, all you can do is let them shoot themself in the foot. If he wants to die in Maryland, I'm not the hero who stops him. Some might say I'm not a hero at all.

I motion to Jay and Enrique. "Help him."

A few minutes later, the lot of them are gone, and Tic Tac lifts a finger. "Houston—"

"Don't say that again," I warn. "What did you find?"

"Mark has a house in the Hamptons. He's a wealthy man, whose company hit big with a weapons patent."

Hamptons wealthy, I think. The kind that could hire an assassin.

"And ouch," Tic Tac adds. "Oh man, I screwed up. I just realized that Mark and Elsa's phones haven't left the ranch in several days. If they're the killers, they aren't carrying their phones with them. Should we tell Ellis?"

"I don't think so," Jack interjects. "He's a dumbass to go to Maryland on his own and shut out Agent Love-Mendez."

Agent Love-Mendez. I'd tell him how stupid he sounds, but he's actually been helpful, and there are other things on my mind. Ellis was a little too eager to take on Maryland himself, without me. What if Marie wasn't the only one with a financial interest in all of this in some way? What if Ellis had one, too?

I reach into my field bag and retrieve Marie's journal. Once I've gloved up, I remove the plastic and I tab through dates. The entire month of April is missing. I toss my gloves and return the journal to the plastic covering before handing it off to Tic Tac. "I found that under Marie Rodriguez's mattress. See what you can do with it." I push to my feet and then announce, "I'm going to the Hamptons," only to have Jack literally cheer.

If irritation kills, this man is going to be the death of me.

Only a few minutes later, I'm in the lobby of the building, intending to hunt down Jay and Enrique, when a familiar man steps in front of me. A man my husband believes would love to see me dead.

"Just who I came to see," he greets in a heavily accented voice. "My new daughter-in-law. It's past time we have a private chat, don't you think?"

CHARACTERS

Lilah Love (28)—dark-brown hair, brown eyes, curvy figure. An FBI profiler working in Los Angeles, she grew up in the Hamptons. Her mother was a famous movie star who died tragically in a plane crash, which caused Lilah to leave law school prematurely and eventually pursue a career in law enforcement. Lilah's father is the mayor of East Hampton; her brother is the Hamptons' chief of police. She dated Kane Mendez against her father's wishes. She was brutally attacked one night, and Kane came to her rescue, somewhat, and what unfolded that night created a secret between the two they can never share with anyone else. This eventually caused Lilah to leave and take a job in LA, away from her family, Kane, and that secret. Lilah is back in the Hamptons now, married to Kane Mendez, and working as part of a special FBI task force to take down the Society— an underground organization with deep pockets, and fingers in all the wrong political pots.

Kane Mendez (32)—brown hair, dark-brown eyes, leanly muscled body. He's the CEO of Mendez Enterprises and is thought to be the leader of the cartel that his father left behind when he was killed. But Kane's uncle runs the operation, while he runs the legitimate side of the business. Lilah's ex from before she left for L.A., and now her husband since they've reconnected.

Director Murphy (50s)—gray hair, perfectly groomed. Former military. Lilah's boss. The head of the L.A. branch of the FBI. Sent Lilah back to the Hamptons to follow an assassin case, then kept her local in NYC working on a cold-case task force. Is known to have had strong feelings for Lilah's mother, and as head of the task force Lilah is on, continues to point her in the direction to take down the Society.

Jeff "Tic Tac" Landers—Lilah's go-to tech guy at the FBI. She's pulled him onto the task force with her.

Grant Love (57)—blue eyes, graying hair. Lilah's father, the mayor, retired police chief of East Hampton. A perfect politician. Charming. He's being groomed by Ted Pocher to run for New York governor.

Andrew Love (34)—blond hair, blue eyes. Lilah's brother and the current East Hampton police chief. Andrew is protective and seems to be the perfect brother. The problem is that he's perfect at everything, including being as macho and bossy as their father. There's more to Andrew than meets the eye. Now an advisor for his father, the future Governor of New York.

Lucas Davenport—tall, and looks like a preppy version of Tarzan. A very successful and good-looking investment banker, and addicted to hacking. He is a cousin of sorts to Lilah and Andrew. His father was the stepbrother of Lilah's father. His father was also known to have been with Lilah's mother, Laura, on the night they both disappeared in the plane crash. He flirts mercilessly with Lilah, seeing as they're not blood-related, but she always shoots him down.

Laura Love—Lilah's mother. Famous actress. Died four years ago in a horrific plane crash, which has now been discovered to be a murder at the hands of the Society. She infamously portrayed Marilyn Monroe in an Oscar-winning performance.

Ted Pocher— A thin, tall man in his fifties, with salt and pepper hair, and an air of arrogance and authority to him, which he wears like a second skin. Billionaire CEO of the world's fifth largest privately held conglomerate, Pocher Industries. Has taken a liking to Lilah's father in hopes of furthering her father's political career. He tried to do business with Kane and Mendez Enterprises but was turned down because of his rep for shady business deals. One of the leaders of the Society.

Jay—Lilah's bodyguard, courtesy of Kane. His voice is heavily accented, ugly scar ripped down his cheek. Thick, dark hair. Has taken a bullet for Lilah. Mexican.

Chief Houston (30s)—NYPD Chief. Lilah's contact when she needs a police presence or liaison while in the city. Lilah knows him from back in the day. Linebacker, fit frame.

Kit—tall, brooding, fit Mexican man who smiles big and used to guard the front desk of Kane and Lilah's building before he became a personal bodyguard for both of them as needed. He kills easily. Kane trusts him.

Jack Cox (36)—Wavy, slick-backed hair, a sculpted but somehow weak jawline, and glasses. Chemist, with a Ph.D. who worked at NYC Health and Hospitals right out of college until last year when he became a forensics tech. Has been stalking Lilah online with a huge mass of people, and tracked her down (by stealing her information from Rollins' Rolodex) to get her involved in the Horror Movie killings.

Ghost—One of the deadliest assassins on the planet. Went up against Lilah once before during her first case back in the Hamptons when she faced off with the Society. Tall, muscular, and confident, his grace is that of a practiced soldier. His dark brown hair is short, but not short enough to read as military. His temples are streaked gray, perhaps thirty-six or seven. Pale green eyes. High cheekbones, straight nose.

Gabriel—One of Kane's men who helps protect him and Lilah. His father worked for Kane for five years. Military background, recently honorably discharged. Sniper.

Enrique—One of Kane's men who helps protect him and Lilah.

Laslo—One of Kane's men who he has dubbed to take over the cartel when Kane can finally get rid of his uncle.

Rich Moore—blond surfer-dude looks, blue eyes. Works with Lilah. He and Lilah were sleeping together until Rich wanted more and Lilah called it off.

Greg Harrison—Lilah's old partner from the New York Police Department. Currently in a lot of hot water with Internal Affairs over an incident that may or may not be of his own making. He was partnered with Nelson Moser prior to being put on leave by IA pending further investigation but has been working independent security with Moser in the meantime.

Roberto Mendez—Kane's father who was supposed to be dead, murdered a few years ago. Came out of hiding when Kane killed his uncle, Miguel, and tried to pass the cartel leadership to another.

Danica "DD" Day—Thirty-something, blonde, used to be a model. Deputy Medical Examiner of Suffolk County. Worked the Wedding Duet murders with Lilah.

Director Ellis—fifty-something, and much like my father—fit, with dark, salt and pepper hair. Also much like my father, he's wearing an expensive suit, but director or not, he shouldn't be able to afford the price tag this one demands.

Calvin Adams—Acting FBI Director. Will oversee Murphy's Society directives. Took over when Director Casey stepped down right as Murphy was murdered. Ex-Special Forces, well decorated, FBI for ten years. Thirty-eight, with sandy-brown wavy hair that is most likely curly but refuses to straighten.

Clyde Walker—His company, Blackhawk Security, held a top-secret government contract for years until the committee being targeted in this case decided to strip him of the contract. He operated out of a ranch in Maryland training snipers, including his daughter, Elsa.

Elsa Walker—Sniper. Daughter of Clyde Walker.

Mark Walker—VP at a firearms company. Son of Clyde Walker.

CHAPTER ONE

Fuck is for: Fuck Kane's father for about ten things, starting with him cornering me in the lobby of my own building for some one-on-one time. I have a murder to solve, not commit, and lives to save, not take, at least for the time being, and sadly, with him showing up here to play bastard and bitch, there's no time to enjoy.

"You're a man of surprising vigor and height considering the news loves to call you short and dead," I say dryly. "I loved it, too, in case you're wondering. The part where you were dead. Not the part where you were short, because that would have made Kane short. I always knew that part was bullshit."

His lips curve as he digests my observation with obvious amusement. He's tall, dark, and, as would be expected considering he's Kane's father, handsome, if not for the fact that he's the leader of a brutal cartel with more than one massacre under his belt.

He wants me dead.

I want him dead.

It would be disrespectful to pretend otherwise, and the Hispanic culture is all about respecting their elders.

"Sadly," I reply to his offer of a little private chat, "I'll need to take a raincheck, as I'll surely kill you if given the chance, and that would be too messy for my present time restrictions." I step around him and manage two steps toward the door.

"Are you so sure it would be you who killed me, bella?"

Bella.

Beautiful.

The name Kane calls me, and there is no question that's by intent. He's letting me know he's more intimately aware of our relationship than he should be.

"You're an FBI agent," he adds.

Now it's my turn to feel the bittersweetness of amusement. I rotate to face him. "Funny thing about my track record wearing a badge. No one ever seems to make it into cuffs. They do, however, make it into a grave. You think the badge will keep me from killing you? You must not know as much about me as you think you do. Sometimes I just enjoy killing a little too much." I smile, sticky-sweet and poisonous.

"Oh fuck," comes a muttered curse from behind, and I whip around to find Enrique standing there, looking as pale as me, and considering I'm a white chick and he's not, that's saying a lot.

"Choose," is all I say to him, and I walk right past him, but by the time I'm at the door, he's by my side.

"I chose a long time ago, Lilah," he says, opening the door for me, "and it pisses me off you don't know that."

He's such a girl, I swear, and if he thinks holding a door for me proves anything, he's not just a girl, he's a dumb girl. Once I'm outside, I find Jay leaning on the door of an SUV. He pops off, straightening, on alert when he brings me into view, and I move his direction.

I do not reach for my phone, certain we're being watched, and that I'm expected to reach for my phone to call Kane in a panic. I'm not in a panic, not one fucking little bit. My dance card is filled with monsters, and I'd call Kane's father just another one of the same, but he's not so simple. His life and death have consequences for both me and, most importantly, Kane.

In fact, he's one big mindfuck for Kane.

I slide into the SUV with Enrique following. The door shuts behind him, but I still don't reach for my phone. This is going to send Kane off the deep end, and he's already there, locked and loaded and ready for a slaughter.

"I'm loyal, Lilah," Enrique states, staring at me with steel in his eyes.

Loyalty is a tricky business. It's rarely about someone else and always about oneself. He knows it. I know it. Jay joins us, and I call out to him. "Airport. Chopper. Hamptons."

"What's going on?" he asks over his shoulder.

"Drive now. Talk later," I say, "and hopefully less than normal."

Jay grunts and does as I say while I settle into my seat, sinking into the leather, but I don't reach for my phone. I don't immediately call Kane. No matter how capable I am of taking care of myself, I'm the line in the sand, and it's been crossed.

Enrique narrows his eyes on me. "Why aren't you calling Kane? He needs to know what just happened."

I lean forward and point at him. "You say you're loyal; you need to leave this to me."

"To Kane first. My job—"

"You need to be clear, and I mean crystal fucking clear, Enrique. Kane is never emotional, but he is now, and emotional actions lead to stupid, risky actions."

"Kane isn't emotional."

"He's human."

He studies me several hard beats. "What do you need from me?"

"I need to be the one who tells him about Roberto visiting me in person, which allows me to gauge his reaction and control his actions."

"A delay is not an option, Lilah. He's Kane Mendez. You know what that means."

"It means a lot of fucked up shit he needs to navigate with a clear head."

"Don't put me in a graveyard position. I cannot hold this back from him. You have to know that."

"Don't be a little bitch, *Enrique*."

"Lilah," he breathes out, gravel in his voice, a plea in the depths of his voice that has me grimacing.

He was Kane's man before he was our man, and Kane's trust in him is the only reason he's here with me right now, or ever. I grit my teeth, drag my phone from my pocket, and dial Kane, who's been MIA for most of the day. I have no doubt this indicates he's on some mission to destroy his father he knows won't win my approval. I'd say he's taking the approach to do the deed and beg for forgiveness later, but he won't bother.

As Enrique stated, he's Kane Mendez.

Considering he's been avoiding me all day, I don't expect him to answer, and he doesn't, and my call lands in his voicemail. "There's been a new development," I tell him via the recording. "Enrique is with me. He feels the need to tell you, and I told him it's something I need to tell you in person. Besides, how would he tell you when you won't fucking answer the phone? We're following a lead to the Hamptons." I hang up and glare at Enrique. "Happy?"

We halt at a stoplight and Jay is leaning around the seat, waving a hand at the rear. "For the love of God, will someone please tell me what's going on?!"

"He's going to call me," Enrique replies tightly. "Watch and see."

My cellphone rings in my hand, and I glance down to find Kane's number. Normally I'd have a smartass remark to make, but there is nothing but dread in my belly. I answer the call. "Kane."

"What do you need to tell me?" His voice is the slice of a steel blade.

"I'm headed to the Hamptons to follow up on a lead."

"You said that in the voicemail."

"Right. Where are you?"

"I'll meet you in the Hamptons. Lilah, what aren't you telling me?"

"A question that seems pretty flipping ironic coming from a man who's avoided me for hours. What aren't *you* telling *me*, Kane?"

I'm greeted with heavy, thick silence.

"Fine. Fuck you, Kane, for pushing me against my best judgment. I need a minute." I grit my teeth, and as we are still not moving, scoot to the door before saying, "Drive around the block and come back and get me." I don't wait for approval or understanding. I exit the vehicle.

Enrique curses, but I'm already outside, where I dodge a car and step onto a crowded sidewalk. By the time I'm there, Enrique has joined me, and I point at him to stay back, glaring as I do. He's the reason I'm about to create a shitshow with Kane, and it's pissing me off.

He's at least smart enough to hold up his hands and stand down. I weave through the crowd and claim a spot out of the range of the crush, next to a chicken restaurant. How appropriate considering Enrique is acting like a true chickenshit, and because why wouldn't I want to have this conversation next to a chicken restaurant?

I shove the phone to my ear again and say, "The only reason I'm doing this is because Enrique is wetting his pants right now, afraid to hold this back from you."

"Tell me."

"Your father tried to corner me in the lobby of our building. I didn't have time for his bullshit, and I handled it."

"More, Lilah," he bites out rather predictively, and I stop fighting him and the inevitable spilling of details.

"He suggested we have some long overdue time together, or some shit like that." I wave my hand in the air. "I told him if I had one-on-one time with him, I'd kill him, and I unfortunately didn't have time for how messy that would get."

"And he said?"

"He said an FBI agent wouldn't kill anyone. You know how this went, Kane. It was short, and I was my normal sweet self. The end."

"More, Lilah," he repeats. "What did you say when he said you wouldn't kill him?"

I sigh heavily. "I told him he doesn't know me well or he wouldn't ask that question."

"And he replied with what?"

"Was I sure it would be me that killed him, not the other way, which we both know was a stupid question. This is me we're talking about."

He's silent again—a thick, dangerous silence that has me saying, "Kane? What are you going to do?"

"He's handled, Lilah."

"How?"

"I'll see you at the house."

"When?"

"I'll let you know." He hangs up.

Holy fuck. He hangs up, and Enrique must know as he marches my direction. I meet him halfway and point at him. "If he ends up dead or in jail over this, you're just dead. Do not even think about joining me for the rest of this trip. I can't tiptoe around what you'll yap about." I step around him just in time to find Jay halting at the stoplight. I rush that way, climb inside, and order, "Drive."

"Enrique?"

"Can go suck a giant banana for all I care. Drive."

He doesn't drive, and horns honk behind us. "Lilah, he means well."

"He just put Kane in danger."

"He didn't intend—"

"He put Kane in danger," I repeat, "and if you aren't smart enough to read between the lines, let me dumb it down for you. He'll catch up, Jay, and with a little time and space, I might let him live. Drive."

Jay accelerates and places us in motion, potentially saving Enrique's life in the process.

CHAPTER TWO

Traffic is at a standstill. Horns honk with no purpose. "Do the idiots think if they make noise, the cars in front of us will miraculously move?"

"They're cranky, I guess," Jay replies.

I grunt.

People say us New Yorkers are cranky all the fucking time. We aren't cranky. The vast majority of us have either had time wasted in traffic and have no time left for bullshit, or we've been forced into the subway, where we try to make eye contact with no one and still end up with a person in a garbage bag harassing us.

"Dumb shit with no purpose is just dumb shit, and it will get you killed, Jay."

"Aren't we talking about traffic?"

"Your point?"

He thrums his fingers on the steering wheel and, after a long stretch of silence, says, "Birthdays are a big thing in my family." He is apparently of the mindset that he must fill the wait time with mindless words. "I had no idea yours was next week." He glances over at me with no concern for traffic, as it's not moving. "I'll bring you a strawberry pie."

"Stop talking," I say, pointing at him.

His expression is pure exasperation. "Okay, what the hell, Lilah? You love strawberry pie. What could I have possibly said wrong?"

I twist around to face him. "This, this right here, is why being trapped in a car with you doesn't work for me. You get me a pie and expect me to let you get killed? I talked to Kane. We're in agreement. You're going to the police academy. If you graduate, you keep your job."

"This is ridiculous, Lilah. I'm on the job, doing the job. And if you want me to do a better job, have someone who thinks like your enemies train me. Have Ghost train me, not the police academy."

I snort laugh. "Ghost would eat you alive."

"Or not. Maybe you underestimate me."

I don't, I think, but he might be onto something. Maybe he does need a killer to train him. I settle back into my seat and think about Enrique. He's a killer. So is Kit. So am I, for that matter, but we're the bust your balls and kick your ass style of trainers that might send Jay to a corner to cry. And the fact that I think he might cry tells me training won't change him. Death will, and why would I wish that on him?

"And for the record," Jay says, "you just admitted you like me, Lilah." He grins.

"Don't make me shoot you."

"I thought you were trying to keep me safe."

"From everyone but me. If you piss me off, I will shoot you, Jay."

Fortunately for him, traffic begins to move and my cellphone buzzes with a text, which includes the address I'll be visiting once in the Hamptons. I use Google Maps and check the location to that of my favorite diner, the one Murphy seems to have named as important.

One mile.

Isn't Murphy clever, I reluctantly concede. Not clever enough to stay alive, but clever. He just let me know I'm headed the right direction, but was he telling me Mark was his killer? I'm not sure he had a chance to pass along that information, and I don't believe in coincidences. At the very least, Murphy was following a lead that led him to Mark.

My brows furrow. *I think.* This doesn't feel right or certain.

I might not believe in coincidences, but the reality here is that we live the same distance from the diner as does Mark. My father and Pocher, not much further.

My bingo moment might not be bingo at all. Damn it to hell and fuck you, Murphy, for dying in the first place without telling me the truth about my mother. I text Tic Tac. *I need pictures of Mark and Elsa. How long has Mark had a house one mile from me? And does Elsa have a place here too or where does she live?*

Hold please, he replies, and a minute later adds, *Elsa lives at the Maryland property her father used for his training facility after she exited the military a year after Clyde's death.*

Is she running it now?

No. She converted it to a firing range. And I've already checked. None of the employees are anything but kids. No assassins in the mix. Mark bought it while you were in LA, and you haven't exactly been social. And don't get pissed, but considering he's in weapons manufacturing, won't Kane know him? Photos should ping any moment along with basic bios.

I'd snap back at him just to enjoy the squirm that would follow, but he's right. Kane will know Mark. And Mark will know Kane, which means he knows who he's married to. The odds that Mark expects me to come after him are next to certain.

I consider texting Kane, but he won't answer, and I don't need him getting his men in between me and Ghost, not when Ghost knows things I need to find out. Besides, he's up to his own no good, or he wouldn't be on silent mode.

My brother might know Mark, but if he dives into this too deeply, he'll end up dead. The other option is Lucas, who's apparently drunk as fuck but might know Mark. He was also hacking for very bad people about the time Mark moved in, which might mean Mark. I try to call him and land in his voicemail, which tells me he's likely passed out. *Damn it, Lucas,* I think, needing to know what he knows before I confront Mark, but I'm not going to have that luxury. Not when I'm racing to get to Mark before Ghost.

The photos ping and I focus on the living; Elsa, who's redheaded, pretty, and thirty-two. She is well decorated from her ten years in the army and had twenty kills overseas. Translation, she is immune to the idea of killing. I wonder who has more kills? Her or Ghost?

***

22

Fifteen minutes later, Lucas hasn't called me back or replied to several texts I've sent him, and Jay has pulled us into the airport. "He obviously took the subway," Jay says, motioning to Enrique where he stands by the door.

"I'd say serves him right, but I'm not sure we had the better trip."

"He needs Kane to trust him, Lilah."

Irritation tics in my jaw. "If he's dead, it won't matter, now, will it?" I reach for the door.

"Lilah," he says firmly.

Jay and firm are not words that go together. Poor DD. But the earnest quality of his voice has me looking back at him. "What, Jay?"

"Kane isn't stupid, and he loves the fuck out of you. He won't die when you're alive. He'll be strategic. You might not like how he approaches solving this problem, but he wouldn't do it if he didn't think it was necessary, either."

There's an unfamiliar emotional twist in my gut, and I find myself softening in a way I prefer not to experience. With a frog in my throat, I can do nothing but offer a choppy nod and exit the vehicle. I believe Kane will fight to live, to protect me, but no one wants to die.

My cellphone rings, and I glance down to where I hold it to find my father calling, the last fucking person I want to talk to right now. I decline the call. I trudge forward to greet Enrique. "Mark Walker. What do you know about him?"

"Tell me more."

"Weapons manufacturer who moved into the Hamptons when I was in California."

"Right. I remember Kane having him checked out way back when. He keeps to himself and has never been a problem. Why?"

"He might have killed Murphy. I need to know what Kane's guy knows."

"I really don't think there was much of a reason for us to dig, but I'll find out."

"Dig now, before we take off. Ghost is hunting this guy and I don't want him dead until I kill him. Make sure he

23

stays alive." With that, I step around him and head inside the airport, hoping like hell that Ghost fears Kane enough to let his men live.

Fifteen minutes later, I've belted up, ready for the peace and quiet of a roaring engine that makes everyone shut their mouths, when my phone pings with a text from an unknown number.

You're late, Lilah. I keep overestimating you.

A chill runs down my spine. I have no question over the identity of my texter. This is Ghost. While I was in traffic, he was on his way to Mark Walker, who I can only assume is dead. That's what Ghost does. He makes people dead.

CHAPTER THREE

Ghost is waiting on me.

He knows I won't send anyone to capture or kill him. And that's not an agreement between killers, but rather a hostage situation, and knowledge is the hostage. He knows who killed Murphy. Therefore, I must protect him.

For now.

I screenshot the number he contacted me on and consider texting it to Tic Tac to research, but think better. Ghost will cover his ass and do it well, and if anyone figures out Ghost is waiting on me, they'll send in the cavalry, and the cavalry will end up dead.

Damn it, I think before I text Ghost: *I'll be there in an hour and a half.*

So slow, he replies. *I'm not sure what to make of that, Agent Mendez.*

He's throwing my new name in my face, accusing me of using it to hide. I don't hide. Saving lives takes longer than taking them. *You're a little too fast for your own good. I bet you made a mistake I can extort, and, of course, I will.*

You have no idea how much time I put into a perfect kill. I'll show you if you want. There's a flirty, threatening tone to the message before he adds, *Should we meet here, or for strawberry pie?*

I tilt my head at the question. How the fuck does he know about the pie? He follows me, I conclude. Of course he follows me, but what pisses me off is that I didn't know that until this moment when he wanted me to know. That's dangerous. He's dangerous. I reply with: *I only eat pie with people I like.*

You like me. And I like you, too. It's why you're still alive.

As if, I think and respond with: *Big egos make big targets.*

Which one of us are you warning?

25

I'll pick up a pie on my way there. We can share it, and I'll know it's not poisonous, but you won't. It's not like I have to hurry. We both know Mark is dead. I needed him, asshole.

I told you I'd take care of this for you. See you soon, Lilah.

Lilah.

Not Agent Mendez.

What kind of fuckery is this?

I curse and check my messages to find nothing. No one has shit for me right now, but Ghost does. The pilot climbs onto the chopper, and I thrum my fingers on my seat, almost immune to the noise vibrating around me—I take this flight so often. Ghost is a cat playing with his prey, and I'm the prey; only I'm not prey. I'm the one who finally kills him. *After* I'm done with him. If he thinks otherwise, good. I can make that work for me. I'm better underestimated.

Enrique is already in the seat next to me, strapping in. I text him to avoid yelling over the rage of the engine. *Have someone pick up a pie to take with me to Mark Walker's.*

I watch him respond to the ping of his phone, and he snaps it from his pocket, reads the message, and scowls at me. "What?" he mouths.

"Just fucking do it," I mouth right back. "And no pie for you." I sink back into my cushion before closing my eyes, certain that bringing Ghost a pie is the way to win over an assassin. And as a bonus, we need a knife to cut it.

CHAPTER FOUR

I step into the Hampton's airport, leaving the thundering of the engine behind me, to find no one waiting on me. Just the way I like it. Of course, Enrique and Jay are still my little stalkers, one at each side of me, while Enrique remains on my last ticking nerve, but I need things from him right now so he can stay.

Halting, they both step in front of me, and I lift a finger at Enrique, a question in the action. "I sent you an email with all we have on Mark Walker," he replies, clear on what I want. He knew what I wanted earlier, too, and didn't give two fucks.

"And?"

"He's filthy rich, but it all seems legit. If it wasn't, he was good at hiding the dirt, and he wasn't important enough to us to dig."

"Who are we talking about?" Jay asks.

"If I tell you, I have to kill you," I say.

"Then why does Enrique know?"

"He's already dead as far as I'm concerned," I say, and without a blink, Enrique's direction, I step around him and head for the door. I don't bother to ask about the pie. If he forgets it, I have an excuse to make him dead to everyone, not just me.

By the time I'm in the back of the SUV with the air cranking, Jay driving, and Enrique staring at me while I ignore him, my cellphone pings with a message from Ghost that reads only: *?*

I reply back with: *?*

You get what you give. He has to use words to get words. *I'm counting on that pie.*

I'm not fucking DoorDash, I reply. *I'll bring the pie, but I want something in exchange.*

I don't negotiate.

Then you can watch me eat the pie. As you know from following me the fuck around, I like it way more than you.

A full minute later, he hasn't replied, and I glance over at Enrique. "The pie?"

"Is waiting on you at Walker's house. Why are you taking him pie?"

"I'm hungry. Why did you need to call Kane? Because, apparently, Kane has you by the balls and there's no blood making it to your brain."

"I have to be loyal to him, Lilah."

"Getting him killed isn't loyalty." Jay pulls the SUV to a halt on the outskirts of the Walker property, just outside a private gate and next to another SUV that will be our men. "We're not done on this topic, but *we are* done." I exit the vehicle, and one of Kane's men I've met before pushes off of the other SUV with a box in his hand. He's a big dude with a bald head and bulky muscles, but not an inch of fat on him, and he wouldn't be working anywhere near me if Kane didn't trust him.

"Lilah," he greets, a twinkle in his eyes as he indicates the pie. "I take it you're hungry?"

"Thanks, Taz," I say, "and I'm always hungry." I claim the box and add, "And I do love this pie, but this time it serves a purpose."

"Raz," he corrects. "Pronounced like Rawz."

My brows furrow. "*Rawz?* What the fuck kind of name is that? Were your parents drunk when they named you?"

He laughs—a deep, down to his belly kind of laugh. "Maybe my great-great grandparents were when they chose it generations back and started the family name. I'm one of four Raz's. It's a play on La Razza, meaning 'the people.' I'm supposed to be a man of the people."

"But why? People suck. I'd offer you pie in condolence, but I like to fatten people up before I kill them, and so far, I don't want to kill you."

His brow shoots up. "Thank you?"

"You're welcome. See? I have manners. Tell everyone. Call them liars if they say differently."

His lips quirk. I entertain him. He might be Enrique's replacement.

Enrique joins us. "The gate is oddly open, which feels off to me."

"The house has been quiet for the past hour," Raz assures him and me.

"The gate is open for me," I say. "I'm expected."

Jay steps to our side now, and I motion to the lot of them. "Stay."

I pull away from them and head for the gate, and freaking Enrique is by my side. I whip around to face him. "I don't know what is up your ass, but I have a job to do. If you get in the way, I'll arrest you or kill you."

"Ghost is up my ass, Lilah. Kane is freaking out over his interest in you."

"You need to check yourself, Enrique, or I'll do it for you. And you clearly cannot be on duty with me. Consider yourself relieved."

"This is not just about Ghost," he says, planting his hands on his hips. "I've seen what Roberto's capable of, Lilah."

"You're acting like a little bitch." *Which is not like him*, I think. "Why?"

"Roberto is a monster."

He has a history with this man, one that's making him nervous, one that might pit him against Kane, and he doesn't know how to fix it. "Just stay. You can confess to me later, and we'll deal with it."

He breathes out. "I'm not sure we can."

"Stay, Enrique." I rotate away from him and walk toward the gate. First Ghost. Then whatever is making Enrique act a fool.

CHAPTER FIVE

Ghost makes a living from the shadows, which makes the fact that the lights are off in Mark Walker's house expected, if not inconvenient. I can't shoot what I can't see, and I can't carry a pie while trying to shoot what I can't see.

My gut says Ghost doesn't want to kill me and really wants this pie, but I also tell myself I'll arrest my next perp instead of killing them, and it doesn't happen. Ghost is a seasoned killer, and it would suck to die while holding a pie I didn't even get to enjoy—at least let me have a full belly—but I go with my gut. I open the door, reaching inside and flipping on the light, using the back of my hand to prevent an overlay of fingerprints, though I'm doubtful Ghost will be stupid enough to leave his behind. It's the other people who visited Walker I want to identify.

The room is illuminated in a warm glow, and I'm greeted by a foyer with a fancy chandelier overhead. Hamptons money loves fancy chandeliers, as if how a lightbulb is displayed validates their existence and everyone can now bow at their feet. Also typical, a stairwell lined with an oriental rug twists and turns in an upward path, with an open archway to my left and a shut door to my right. It's the shut door that sets me on edge—the kind of place the boogie man hangs out and waits on you, but Ghost wouldn't hide from me.

That would make him appear weak when I've already become some sort of weakness for him, even if he doesn't know it, though I suspect he does. Weak isn't dumb. It's human, something I suspect he's feeling for the first time in a very long time.

I walk left, carefully flipping on another light to find myself in a sitting room with a shiny black grand piano in my direct line of sight, and it's not exactly clean and tidy. A man I can only presume to be Mark Walker is lying across it on his back, his head hanging off to face me, a bullet between his eyes, blood dripping crimson on the cream-colored carpet.

I'm aware of Ghost sitting on the couch to my right, but I remain focused on Mark, on the perfectly placed bullet, on the degree of congeal to the blood that tells me he's been here for hours. It's a dangerous, bold move, and I wonder if it was all for this time with me.

And if so, why?

"Is that the pie?"

He needs my attention, can't stand not having it, and even expects and craves it. I rotate on him and scowl, aware of his uncovered face, a handsome forty-something face with a chiseled jawline and high cheekbones fitting of a model, not a killer. Dahmer would be jealous. When I saw him before he wore a hoodie, shadows on his face, nighttime in his favor. I had him drawn and it was completely wrong which is curious. How was I this wrong?

There's expectancy in his expression, a desire to strike fear in me when I realize this means he plans to kill me. Instead, I feel relief. In a world filled with games, we're done playing them, at least after tonight. One of us will not leave this house alive.

I like it.

It works for me.

I dive right in and admonish him, flicking my chin at Mark Walker's dead body. "Could you not have waited until I asked him a few questions? I mean, *fuck,* Ghost. I need to know what he knows about Murphy."

As if I don't know he's going to try to make me dead; therefore, the facts are irrelevant. As if I'm not going to make him dead. "Maybe I know what you need to know."

His gaze is steady, perhaps deceptively steady, but there is no doubt he knows a lot more than most, or I wouldn't be doing this stupid dance with him. I cross to join him, sitting down and noting the plates and silverware already present. I open the box in my lap, remove the pie, and toss the container before setting the prize on the table between us.

I reach for the butter knife he's set out and hold it up. "I prefer a sharper blade. It's less messy."

"A blade is messy."

I flash back to me on top of Roger, stabbing him over and over, blood splattering all over me. "Depends on how it's used."

"Based on experience?"

"Knowledge."

His eyes narrow. "Knowledge?"

"That's right," I say, and that's all he gets, not that it really matters what I say. One of us is already dead, and it's not me.

He seems to think better than to push. "As a woman, I'd think a blade would be less effective than a firearm."

"Shooting someone's rather boring, don't you think?" I dig the blunt blade into the pie and hit the shell with no success, setting it back down on the table "We need a proper knife."

"I'll get one," he says, pushing to his feet and rounding the coffee table before offering me his back, essentially telling me he sees me as no threat. He assumes that as a law enforcement officer I won't shoot him in the back, but he forgets the name Mendez really is gangster, and I'm the one who put burying a body on the "to do" list.

He's tall, which I noticed during our last encounter, lean, fit. He disappears through a doorway, and I reach down and scoop whipped cream onto my finger. I'm not letting Ghost ruin this pie for me, and I give the sweetness a taste, allowing it to linger on my tongue, along with the idea of ending Ghost once and for all, and it tastes good, really damn good.

So does the whipped topping.

Ghost returns and saunters toward me, a loose-legged swagger about him that manages to be as casual as it is predatory. He sits across from me and offers me the steak knife, butt first, telling me I'm not a threat. I accept it, and I swear there is something about me and a blade that's far too deliciously deadly.

Ghost sees it too, feels it, and for the first time since I arrived, there's a flicker of uneasiness in him. He now knows what he's suspected. Kane isn't the only killer in our family. And Ghost isn't the only killer in the room.

CHAPTER SIX

A slow smile tugs at my lips, and I flip the knife upright, pointing at the sky where the good Lord is looking down on us and asking how he got us so wrong and yet this moment oh so right. The truth is, I might be a flawed creation, but there are few people who could sit across from a monster and feel no fear.

In this moment, the way I am makes sense to me. I lean into it. Embrace it. I was *made* to kill this man.

"*This* is much better," I say in approval of the shiny silver knife. I give it an admiring look and add, "Nice and freshly sharpened—just the way I like my blades, though properly funneled rage tends to overcome a dull blade."

I slice into the pie, and the blade all but turns the crust into butter. I decide it's time to give more thought to the quality of the blades I carry while somehow convincing Kane that it doesn't mean I'll be more likely to use them, but rather more likely to stay alive.

I cut two pieces of pie and set them on the two small plates Ghost has thoughtfully provided—proof even an assassin is thoughtful when it comes to food. I hand a plate to Ghost. "It's delicious, and don't worry about poison. I'm not that discreet."

There's a flicker in his eyes that fades quickly, a reaction that spells transparency that a man who is a ghost wouldn't be in a position to reveal, but he's allowed me the chance to see beneath the sheet, to memorize every inch of his existence. His eyes are green. There's a mole on his left cheek and the scar on his right. His white skin so freshly tanned tells me he's recently spent time in a tropical location, or his home state is sunny year-round.

He accepts the plate, sets it in front of him, and picks up a fork. "Let's try this pie you love so much."

"You followed me around and watched me eat it but didn't actually try it?"

His lips twitch with my reference to him stalking me. He's amused. I am not. "This will be the first time," he confirms.

I set the knife down within reach, feeling as possessive as a lover about that blade, but settling for a fork for now. "Maybe next time you should just sit down with me instead of hiding," I suggest and scoop a bite.

"I don't hide," he says, taking a bite before adding, "I observe. Understanding my prey allows me to exterminate them effectively."

He just called me prey and expects me to cower. Go on with yourself and think that shit. I snort. "Right." With that dismissal, I add, "Have you tried a pencil?"

He scowls. "What?"

"It's an excellent weapon, proven by John Wick. You did watch *John Wick*, right?"

"A movie isn't reality."

"No, but the way he killed with a pencil was pretty badass. And it's kind of the perfect weapon. You can burn it or just shred it, and there's no evidence." I motion toward him with my fork. "Do you like the pie?"

He tilts his head and then sets his fork down. "I don't want to kill you, Lilah."

Lilah again, as if this is personal. It's not. "And yet, I want to kill you," I confess, "but not until I get what I want from you, and you know it."

He narrows his gaze on me. "You really are a killer, aren't you?"

"You waited until you were alone with me to figure this out?"

"I'm bigger than you, in case you didn't remember that devastating detail."

"A very small gun can kill a very big man, in case you've forgotten that devastating detail, though I don't favor my firearm." My brows dip in thought. "And I don't believe I've killed anyone who wasn't to date. No. They were all much bigger. Well, there was one woman. The rest were men."

"You're an FBI agent."

"Kane's father said the same thing to me earlier today, as if I wouldn't kill him because of my badge."

"I thought he was dead."

"He faked it. For now. That won't last. But back to my point: while it's true that it's not encouraged that I kill everyone who crosses me, I'm better at that than I am making arrests. And what they don't know won't kill them, right?" I scoop another bite of pie. "Damn, I love this pie," I murmur and then add, "Kane is growing weary of the cleanup, though, so I'm trying to do better."

"Okay, then, if that's true, why do you kill?"

"Not for money. I have money. So do you now, so we both know that's not why you continue to kill."

"I want more money."

"You enjoy the rush of it," I correct. "For me, well, I blame my father. I crossed the people trying to put him in power, and he agreed to allow them to get rid of me. I'm not sure if he meant for them to drug and rape me too, but while they tried, Kane showed up and pulled him off of me." I swipe whipped cream from the pie onto my finger. "He wanted to question him, but rage won and I stabbed him. Excessively, per Kane. He hid the crime so I wouldn't lose my badge. I blamed him, left him, and then came back to do it all over again. Some think my badge protects him when the truth is he protects my badge."

"And what did your father say when you confronted him?"

"When I found out it was him years later, he told me that I deserved it."

His jaw tics, and I think I see anger in the depths of his eyes. I've hit a nerve, and it's not about my story, but his. "You want me to kill him?" he offers.

"Why would I give you what will bring me joy?"

"Because killing a father isn't like killing anyone else."

Another telltale sign this is about him, not me. "I need him alive."

"Why?"

"Because I need everyone in the Society dead. Where he goes, they go."

He picks up his fork and takes a bite of the pie. "Impossible."

"Nothing is impossible."

He sets his fork down again. "They're as good at hiding as I am, and I'm pretty fucking good."

"And the closer my father gets to the White House, the closer they'll get to him."

"True," he says, "but do you really want to let your father get that close to that kind of power?"

"I like the idea of snatching it right out of his hands. What do you know about Murphy?"

"I don't."

"Then how did you know about Walker?"

"Only what's necessary. I don't have a moral compass that requires I check off a box to do a job."

"Was this a job?"

"Call it whatever you want."

He's not giving me much here. "Did he kill Murphy?"

"I don't know and I don't care. One of them did, so they both need to die."

"To give you your number one killer status."

"Assassin," he amends.

I ignore the comment that drives home the ego behind his actions. "Where's the sister now?"

His lips quirk. "She thinks she's hiding."

"Where is she?" I repeat.

"I don't know, and that's the beauty of the hunt."

He knows, I think.

He pushes to his feet, and I follow, discreetly sliding the blade into my palm and hiding it at the back of my thigh. "Why'd you tell me your secret, *Lilah*?"

Still Lilah, not Agent Love or Mendez, and this time he says my name as if it's silk on his tongue, foreplay to his intent to kill me. "The same reason you've made no effort to conceal your face."

"You've seen me before."

"You look different. You're...different. And you know it. Whatever you showed me in the past wasn't this you."

"I have different versions of me for different people."

"And this is the real you."

"Is it?"

"I think it is. We both came in here with the assumption one of us wouldn't be walking out of here alive. Why hide in that situation?"

His lips curve slightly, his eyes dark with a lusty hunger that only a killer has for death. Let him hunger, but in the end, he'll be a body Kane gets to bury. Seconds tick by, heavy in their implications and promise of violence.

The coffee table separates us, a barrier of little consequence to me, the sweet strawberry pie sitting on its surface with berries as red as his blood soon to be spilled. I *will* kill him, and the narrowing of his eyes tells me he sees that truth in mine; he recognizes the killer I am and denies every moment it doesn't suit me.

It suits me now.

"If I wanted you dead, you'd be dead," he assures me.

"Are you sure? You are only the number two assassin in the world right now. I think it takes the number one assassin to kill me."

He chuckles. "Ouch. That almost hurt. I like you, Lilah. I'm not going to kill you. I'm going to do you a favor instead. When I get my number one status back, I'm going to kill your father."

He's barely made the statement when the lights go out.

CHAPTER SEVEN

My first instinct when slammed into darkness is to yank the blade at my thigh in front of me and take several long backward steps. Movement creaks near the kitchen, and I know he's running. Ghost is freaking running. In darkness lie chickenshit assassins. What the hell is it with all the chickenshit men in my life right now?

Still, I don't move, listening for more movement, waiting for a trap. I mean, the dude is the second highest-rated assassin in the world. A full soundless two minutes tick by, and the lights flicker and illuminate the room. I don't bother hiking it after Ghost. He's gone. The cameras are off, and as my eyes land on the coffee table, I find the pie and all plates and utensils are also gone. Damn it to hell.

I snake my phone from my pocket and dial my brother, who answers on the first ring. "What's happening?"

"You are, or you aren't still chief?"

"Don't be a smartass, Lilah. You know I am."

"You bought a place in New York City."

"What do you want, Lilah?"

"I need a team to Mark Walker's place. He's dead. And yes, it's another assassination."

He curses. "On my way." He hangs up.

Always calm and cool under pressure, my brother. No wonder my father wants him by his side. I set the knife down, open my bag at my hip where it's rested since the airport, and glove up before bagging the knife. It's the only thing Ghost touched and left behind. It's a stupid mistake, which tells me he knows his prints aren't in the system. Thus the nickname, Ghost.

I'm not handing it over to law enforcement, and therefore, it goes straight into my bag. I'm sure my father would approve. I'm trying to catch the assassin that promised to kill him, which hasn't quite sunk in, nor have I decided if I plan to stop him or not.

For now, I stay in the moment, lifting the coffee table up and out before squatting, scanning for a hair or fiber. I don't find any, but the forensic team will have the ability to see what I cannot. Ghost has to know that was a risk of hanging out at a crime scene, but I suspect DNA doesn't worry him. He's unknown to law enforcement—the true number one assassin for a reason. He's a rockstar at killing people. And yet, he didn't try to kill me. I'll contemplate why later.

We won't find Ghost from anything he left behind today, and why the hell he's decided to be my savior by killing my father I do not know, nor do I look forward to telling Kane.

"Lilah!"

At the sound of Enrique's voice, I rotate and call out, "Stop right now!" I quickly cross the room as he curses and appears in the doorway. "Why the fuck are you inside my crime scene without my permission?"

"The lights went out. You said Ghost—"

"Fuck me, when did you turn into the grandma next door, afraid of the boogeyman? And now your prints are on the door. You're here before law enforcement has logged the crime scene. Now you'll have to be registered, printed, and talked to, or you become a suspect. Neither of us needed that complication tonight."

He curses and scrubs his jaw. "Fuck."

"Yeah. Fuck."

He grits his teeth and lifts his chin toward the body. "What happened in here?"

"He was tired and took a nap. What do you think happened in here? As social media likes to say, he got unalived." I dig out a pair of gloves, complete my path to stand in front of him, and slap him in the arm with them. "Put them on and help me search the place before Andrew and his team get here. Unless you want me to unalive you."

He accepts the gloves and pulls them on. "We both know you know who did this, so what are we looking for?"

"It's as if you don't follow me all the time," I snipe. "Or maybe you just don't pay attention unless it's Kane talking. I'm not sure how that keeps either of us safe."

"Lilah," he breathes out. "I was just—"

I cut him off. "Society bullshit, and that includes anything Murphy." I'm already walking away, heading toward that closed door I'd bypassed earlier that I'm betting is a private office. A few steps later, I discover the door is locked and grunt before calling out, "Enrique!"

He appears almost instantly, his brow arched in silent question. "Be a good criminal and break into the door." I jiggle the knob.

He scowls. I ignore him. "My time is limited here. Call me when it's open." I hurry off and do a cursory look around, lingering in the bedroom, searching under the mattress, inside pillowcases, and under the nightstand.

It's on the bottom of a bottle of Advil that I find what looks like a phone number. He didn't put it in his phone for a reason. And he didn't trust himself to remember it either, which means he didn't dial it often or at all. I pull the taped note off the bottle, shoot a photo, and send it to Tic Tac without an explanation when I hear, "Lilah!"

Wonderful. My pain-in-the-ass brother is already here. Enrique fails again. I stick the paper in a sealed bag before it goes in my bag, but don't rush downstairs. What's the point? Enrique failed and clearly isn't as gangster as he pretends.

I walk into the closet and start checking pockets, but find nothing of interest. My phone buzzes with a text from Tic Tac: *It's a burner phone that's presently located in Mark Walker's house.*

"Holy hell," I murmur and check my call log. It's the same number Ghost has been texting me from.

I rush down the stairs to find my brother waiting at the bottom, and I bypass him, ignoring him, as I walk to the couch and kneel beside it. I punch the number into my phone, which Ghost has communicated on, and a cell rings beneath the couch. I bend down and retrieve it, aware that Ghost has just won the game, at least this round.

I'm questioning why Mark has his number, which, of course, was Ghost's intention. Ghost claimed he didn't kill the directors, but what if he did? And if he took the jobs, if Mark and his sister were paying him, why did he kill Mark? Did he kill Mark? Or was he here to save him?

Did the sister hire him to kill Mark?

In which case, is he really, truly still the number one assassin in the world and on the way to kill my father?

CHAPTER EIGHT

I pocket the phone and push to my feet to find my brother and Enrique standing in the room behind me, staring at me. "Is the door unlocked?"

Enrique goes all thin-lipped on me while Andrew offers what he thinks is a salutation. "I told him our guys can handle it."

If I could remember the Spanish curse Kane favors, I'd mutter it now, but I can't. Because I don't want to. Because it's usually used in relation to me. Since Enrique needs to have Little Bitch written across his forehead right now, I motion to my brother and then walk through the doors where Ghost disappeared, which delivers me to a fancy chef's kitchen. The island is huge. The pans dangling above it shiny and fancy. The granite on the counter is an impressive smoke shade with black lines streaked throughout it. Does Mark have a wife who cooks or a housekeeper? Or does he blow things up and then whip up fancy veggies no one will ever eat? And why am I here and don't know any of this?

I whirl around as Andrew joins me. "We have a situation, big brother. Ghost was here."

"As in the assassin? Do I need to lock down?"

"Not us."

He squints at me. For a relatively decent-looking guy, he squints a lot—ugly squints, like the sun is in his eyes. "What does that mean?"

"It means that as I sat down to share pie with Ghost—"

"What the fuck do you mean, as you sat down to share pie with Ghost?"

"Irrelevant outside of the fact that he took my pie and I somehow made him want to kill Dad. He vowed to kill him as soon as he's the number one assassin again, which is tricky since I'm fairly certain he's that now. And always. He was always number one."

Andrew slashes his hands through the air. "Backup. Why does he want to kill Dad, aside from him being a piece of shit? Dad. Not Ghost. Or maybe both."

"He thought I wouldn't kill him because I'm an FBI agent, and—"

"Which would be a normal assumption, if you weren't you. He has no idea what it's like to have a sister who's basically Dexter in high heels."

"Okay, smartass. I'm not Dexter. I'm an FBI agent bad at arresting people."

"Because you kill them."

"Which is what I told Ghost."

"How did Dad come into the picture?"

"I wanted him to understand how easily I could kill him, so I described Kane pulling the guy Dad sent after me off of me and what ensued."

"Meaning what?"

"I stabbed him over and over and over until Kane pulled me off of him."

"Why would you tell him that? Now he has that over your head."

"Because neither of us thought the other was going to leave alive. And I fully believe he meant to kill me, as I did him, but then something about Dad sending that man after me hit a nerve with him."

"Does he know Dad?"

"I'm not sure if it's about Dad or something personal to Ghost that makes him relate."

"Okay. I wouldn't have seen this coming. He could be on his way to kill Dad now."

"Yes, but I think he's far more likely to kill the sister first. Elsa. Unless his wording was meant to trick me."

"Why warn us if that's the case? We have time to protect Dad."

"I doubt he thinks we want to protect him."

He breathes out long and hard. "Do we?"

I almost laugh, but the drama that would cause with Andrew would not be worth it, at least not in our present circumstances. "Where's my choir boy brother?"

"Dead," he says. "He's dead. What are we going to do?"

Enrique pokes his head into the room. "I got the door open."

I glance at Andrew. "We'll talk later."

He eyes Enrique. "We're not done."

"Okay," Enrique says, but he doesn't move.

I have to admire his stubbornness under my ire, even if it is the end of him. "He's fine," I say to Andrew, "and too stupid to be a problem."

"Fuck you, Lilah," Enrique snaps.

"Fuck you, too, Enrique." I whirl on him and place myself between him and Andrew. "Fuck you, all the way to the damn grave where I'm going to put you if you ever pull that shit again."

"I was being loyal."

"To yourself. If you were loyal to Kane, or me for that matter, you'd have risked Kane's wrath to protect him. And he would have understood. Go start searching the room you just opened."

He stares at me several beats, not a waiver to his gaze, and then turns and walks out of the room. I rotate to face my brother. "What was that all about?"

"Focus on the case."

He looks like he wants to push, but seems to get the priorities. Small miracles do happen, like me allowing Enrique to keep breathing. I'm angrier with him than either of us realized, or I'd be past it now. I am not. "Did Ghost kill Mark Walker?" Andrew asks.

"Yes," I say, certainty filling me that I'd lacked earlier. "His presence was him taking credit for the kill. He doesn't want what he doesn't earn, but you won't find proof."

"Why was he here?"

"He wanted to taste my strawberry pie." I motion to the door. "Let's go work the scene." I start walking.

He catches my arm. "Lilah. Why was Ghost here?"

"I already told you. To kill me."

"You told me neither of you thought both of you were leaving, but I assumed that was because you surprised each other."

"My relationship with Ghost is complicated, Andrew. I've got it handled."

"Does Kane know just how complicated?"

"Are you serious right now? Does Kane know? This from the brother who wanted to throw him in jail only six months ago?" I'm out of patience for my fickle brother and his likes and dislikes. I jerk away from him and exit the kitchen.

A new ME I don't know is already examining the body, and I really don't care at this point. Nothing worth knowing is going to be discovered. The only juicy bit I've seen on this crime scene thus far is Ghost and the phone he left behind for me to locate. I wonder if he was testing me to see if I'd find it before the team got here. I wonder if he thinks I'm stupid enough to carry it around with me and allow him to track me.

I walk past the ME without a word and find Enrique waiting for me beside the door he's opened. There's a smug look on his face as I pass the door and stare at an empty room. No one locks an empty room unless the room has a secret.

CHAPTER NINE

At this point, the forensics team is on scene, and I ensure the room is on their radar, but I'm in no rush. Whoever scrubbed the space was over-the-top thorough. We won't find anything, and knowing a cleanup job took place doesn't tell us the story we need told, but I do wonder if Mark put up a fight and Ghost called in some sort of cleanup team.

With this in mind, I leave Enrique lingering by the front door and walk toward my brother. He's chatting with the ME, who's a tall, gym rat of a dude who looks like a Ken doll. And Ken playing with dead bodies makes him a creepster to me. He's a secret serial killer; he has to be.

"Lilah, this is Oliver," my brother says as I join the two of them. "Oliver, this is my sister, Agent Lilah Love."

"Mendez," I say, just to irritate my brother. "The name is Mendez. I married my gangster boyfriend, remember?"

Oliver laughs. "Gotta love the sibling dynamic. I have one myself. She irritates the fuck out of me, and yet I still love her."

"I hate him," I say, but I don't hate Oliver quite as much as I expected, not so far. My ability to hate runs far and wide.

"Oh, I hate her as much as I love her," he says, and it's as if he's right there in my head, plucking words out for his own use. Fuck. Hate. "That bitch," he continues, "just invited my mother over for a weekend at my place without asking me first, which would be fine if my mother wasn't the meanest person I've ever known."

"You just met me," I say. "Don't write me off yet." I don't allow Andrew a chance to agree, moving on with, "How long has he been dead?"

"Three hours max."

Which accounts for my travel time and Ghost's boredom while waiting on my arrival. "Was the body moved?" I ask, and if he doesn't have a fast answer, he's a dumbass, and his endearing foul language won't matter. He'll be dead to me.

"Of course," he preens. "Logically, no one gets shot and lands on a piano that fucking high. He was moved fast, though, before rigor set in."

I eye my brother. "We have a locked room that was wiped clean, not a stitch of furniture. Even the electric plugs were taken out."

"What about the floor?" Andrew asks. "Is it carpet?"

"Hardwood," I say, eyeing Andrew, who says, "Of course, we'll rip it up. But I'm not optimistic we'll find anything when it's been cleaned as precisely as you describe."

"On that note," Oliver interjects, his brows knitting together, "why was cleanup even needed in another room?"

"You said the body was moved," Andrew argues. "I assume that meant he got shot in that room."

"This was a precise hit, a bullet between the eyes. The blood spatter is right next to the piano. The victim was lifted but not moved across the room. Furthermore, the blood spatter wasn't cleaned up."

"Then whatever happened in that room was unrelated to today's kill."

"I can't say it was unrelated," Oliver amends, "but it wasn't where this man was murdered." His attention lands on me. "Were the other victims posed? That's an act of a serial killer mentality, not that of a paid-for-hire assassin."

"They were not," I state.

"That's quite odd," he replies. "Why pose this one?"

"Because this isn't the same guy," I say easily, now certain that Ghost told me the truth. He didn't kill the first two victims. He killed Mark to make him the number two assassin. "And he has nothing to do with whatever happened in that room. For all we know, it's the start of a remodel."

I motion for Andrew to step away from Oliver with me. Oliver takes a hint. "I'll get back to work." He offers us space we don't have to claim.

"Who else lived in the house?"

"No one since his wife left him about six months ago," he says, "but of course, there's a housekeeper who just so happens to be in Europe."

Of course, she is. "Get her on the phone and find out what used to be in the locked room to the right of the front door. And I need an address on the ex."

"That would be Maine."

"Then get me a phone number."

Enrique finds his way back to my side, and I cut him a look, reading the dread on his face. "What?"

"Kane's here."

I rotate to face him. "Did you tell him about Ghost?"

"I told him."

I whip around to face off with my brother. "Say what?"

"I told him. He needs to know just how obsessed Ghost is with you. You brought him a pie. That's not normal, Lilah."

"The pie was for Ghost?" Enrique demands incredulously.

Ignoring him is the theme of the day, and I do it now, my ire directed at my brother. "Thank you, Andrew. Thank you so fucking much."

"You're not invincible, Lilah."

"Neither are you, Andrew. You're on dangerous ground."

"You're threatening me?"

"Snitches get stitches. I'll beat your ass later. For real." I cut away from him, and he catches my arm.

"Dad—"

"He'll kill the sister first."

"Where is she?"

"That's the question of the hour. How about you use those God-given investigative skills and find that out? Unless he forgot to give you those skills and you've been faking it?"

"You're such a bitch."

"So are you, Andrew."

With that, I rotate away from him and exit the house, where my husband is apparently waiting on me. Good. It's time to define the meaning of husband and wife, my way.

CHAPTER TEN

Jay is waiting on me on the other side of the yellow tape Andrew's team has placed around the perimeter of the property, which some fool placed with a wide as fuck girth. I had to walk a freaking mile to duck under the tape.

"Why are you bundled up like an Eskimo?" I ask, referencing the huge-ass puffer jacket he's presently wearing. "And why is it orange and shiny?"

"Easier for you to find me, which we both know is always your priority. Some guy gave it to me. He wouldn't give me an official jacket. Just you." He hands me a black jacket that I can tell has some sort of police logo on it, and it's actually cold enough despite my joking that I accept. "Aren't you a smartass tonight?" I ask, not wanting an answer, as I slide into the jacket.

"You heard?" he asks, and, of course, I know what he means.

"I heard," I say, and I start moving toward the gate. "Where is he?"

"Just outside the gate," he says, confirming I'm headed the right direction. "And it's not good, Lilah. He's not good. He looks like stone that's somehow caught fire."

"That's normal for Kane, Jay."

"There's nothing normal about that man on a good day. Today makes normal levels of 'not normal' look normal. Is this about his father? Is war brewing?"

I halt and face him, lifting a finger as I do. "Calm down. Kane can handle his father."

"Can he? He showed up at the building, at *your home*. My job is to protect you. I need to know what the fuck is going on."

My brow lifts. "Did you really say fuck?"

"I'm not the boy scout you act like I am."

"Not anymore. You've been hanging out with me too much."

"Maybe I haven't been hanging out with you enough. I can handle the shit going on if I know how deep we're going to stick our feet to get to the other side." His voice is one octave above average, and I can all but feel his heart thundering in his chest.

Roberto's return has everyone on our team rattled, and Jay's showing it. No, I think, amending that thought. Enrique is as well. That's why he's overreacting to my normal fucked-up life. The operative word, as Jay has pointed out, being our version of 'normal.' "If Roberto wanted to kill me," I reason, "he would have approached our encounter in a different way. That back there was a game of intimidation, and he lost the game. Now, set that bastard aside and make yourself useful. Go to a diner and get me another pie, then whip on over to the grocery store and grab chocolate and a bag of Lay's potato chips. A girl can't live on all sugar. And water. I need to do something healthy for my body tonight."

"You're sending me to the store, Lilah? Really? I'm not your housekeeper."

"Which is why I am not asking you to scrub my toilet. That would be inappropriate and rude. And I never want to be those things to you, Jay." I grab his arm and squeeze. "Go, please. You need to step back and breathe a minute. If you don't want to run the errands, get in the truck and wait on me."

"I'll wait. I'll DoorDash all your stuff while I'm in the truck."

"Way to be resourceful," I approve.

There's a glint of suspicion in his eyes. "What happened to the other pie?"

"Ghost took it," I say. "Which is why you should get in the truck."

"Ghost was here?"

"Yes. Ghost was here."

"And Kane knows?"

"Because my dumbass brother told him."

For a Mexican, he's really damn white right now. "Is he still here?"

"I doubt it, and I wouldn't fret much either way. He knows I'll kill him if he kills you."

"Then I'd be dead, Lilah," he points out.

"Maybe you should go get that pie."

"I'm escorting you to Kane."

"Okay, hero. Have it your way." I start walking.

He falls into step with me, and for once, his lips are sealed while his hand is on his weapon, as if he'd ever get the chance to see Ghost before he killed him. But Jay's focused, just the way I like him, and I won't tease him out of the behavior I'm trying to train into him. Or beat. I'll beat it into him before I let him die.

We reach the gate, and I spy a black SUV I'm certain to be Kane's transportation. "Stay here," I order, but even as I pull away from him, I can feel Jay at my back, lingering and watching, worried about me. I just can't seem to scare that man off. I can scare him. Just not off.

I round the corner to find Kane leaning on the SUV, with Kit next to him. A splash of relief washes over me, just seeing him alive and well, but anger crushes tenderness, and my wrath will soon be his hell. Today has been about secrets. Defiant secrets that conflict with who we were supposed to be at this point in our relationship, in our marriage.

The minute Kit spies me, he pushes off the vehicle and walks toward the rear. Smart man, avoiding a death sentence, at least for the moment, depending on what role he played in whatever bullshit Kane's not just plotted but acted on. The bullshit he knew I wouldn't approve of. He took the 'sin and ask for forgiveness later' strategy, which is a good way to get divorced or dead.

Because there is no doubt he's been busy creating new enemies when we're already swimming in a sea of monsters.

I head his direction, and he stares at me, watching every step I take, doing so with the intensity of a man who can kill as easily as he can make passionate love to me. He's unreadable and unbelievably bold for coming here tonight.

He's also left the suit behind for black jeans and a black sweater, and despite the bitter cold, he hasn't bothered with a coat. He looks wholly male and arrogantly in control. Good thing he has me to remind him he *is not*. I close the space between us, ready for battle, but the minute I'm in front of him, his hands are on my waist, and I'm pulled hard against him.

"What the fuck are you doing, *woman?* My father and Ghost in one day?" His voice, his eyes, level me with his torment.

His love for me, his fear and worry, punch at me as surely as do his sins. Sometimes I'm reminded I'm human, and those times are always with Kane. I both love that about us and hate it, too. My body softens, and I relax against him, my hand on his hard chest, the beat of his heart thundering beneath my palm. "I didn't come to them. They came to me."

He catches my shoulders and eases me back to meet his stare. "Tell me."

That soft command hardens me. Oh yes, it does. He dares demand answers when he gives me none, avoids me plenty, and knows damn well, just as I do, it's for the wrong reasons. He knows he did something today I won't approve of, now or ever. "Tell you what, Kane, you and your fucking secrets today say you don't have the right to do anything but apologize before and after you explain yourself."

"I won't apologize for doing what I need to do to protect you, Lilah."

I shove out of his arms, and I'm back to pointing, this time at the man of my dreams and nightmares. "Do not even try that bullshit with me, Kane. I can protect myself, as you well know. And we talked about this. I won't live in a world of secrets, no matter how hard the truth is."

He just stares at me, the glint in his eyes just what Jay said—stone and fire. "What happened with Ghost?"

"Not here. None of this is happening here. I have to go back inside and manage the crime scene."

He pushes off the vehicle and instantly closes the minute space I've placed between us, but he's smart enough not to touch me, or he'd have a knee to bend him over right now. "What happened with Ghost?"

"He's going after Mark Walker's sister, who assassinated Murphy. It's a game to him. Who gets there first."

"Ghost doesn't play games."

"He must be bored. What did you do today, Kane?"

"What you suggested, bella. I found a way to control my father."

Now it's my turn to command him. "Tell me."

And his turn to show his defiance. "No."

"No?"

"No, Lilah."

Fury bubbles inside me, and betrayal knives me from within. "That breaks our vows to each other." I jerk hard on my arm and put my own wide girth between us before I say, "I won't be home tonight." With that, I turn and start walking.

"I'll be wherever you are."

I don't turn. I don't humor his arrogance. He can try to find me. He'll fail. Just as he failed to keep his secret. He smells of cigars, exactly the brand the patriarch of the Italian mob smelled of when Kane tied him up in my garage.

CHAPTER ELEVEN

The fucking mob? Now we're in bed with the Society, the cartel, *and* the mob. We're fucked with a capital F. So fucking fucked that we can never be fucked to this degree ever again. Because we will have to kill them all or die. That's where this is going. I hope Kane has his shovel ready.

I need that pie. And chocolate. And for reasons I can't explain, Cheetos. The puffed kind. Knowing those things are in my future is the only thing keeping me from turning around, charging at Kane, and slapping him.

Because he hates to be slapped.

But he deserves so much more.

I also need to know where Mark's sister, the trained sniper, is before she kills someone else, if she's the assassin, though it appears that way. I snag my phone and try to dial Ellis, who went to Maryland looking for her, only to land in his voicemail. The more I think about him leaving for Maryland alone, the more it sits like shit on my shoes. Dirty. Stinky. Bad.

He was on the committee. He could easily have voted to strip Elsa and Mark's father, Clyde, of his contract. And that action is why Clyde is reported to have committed suicide. And where the hell is Adams? He's the acting FBI director and completely MIA.

I round the corner where Jay is waiting on me, and I swear seeing him—normal, kind Jay—infuriates me all the more, and not at him. At Kane. We have people who count on us, who live on the same wavelength and die just the same.

I really have too many men pissing me off right now.

"That didn't look like it went well," Jay observes, and I must glare at him because he holds up his hands as if to ward off my wrath. Kane has all of my wrath right now, and unless he does something as stupid as Kane, he's safe. Or as stupid as himself, for that matter, considering he jumped in front of a damn bullet for me. "You know what happens to nosy people, Jay?"

"Do I want to know?"

"Death is too gentle a punishment," I assure him and start walking.

He drops back and then hurries to fall into step with me. "That was extreme."

"I am extreme. If you don't know that by now, there's no helping you."

"The pie and groceries are being delivered," he says, clearly knowing me well enough to know that food is a safe haven. He's going to love it when I tell him we have to go to the diner anyway. I might have talked myself into believing that card for the diner Murphy left for me was just a card to a great place with strawberry pie, if not for the missing employee.

"Unlock the SUV," I order, already rounding the hood and heading toward the passenger door. By the time I'm there, it's open, and I climb inside.

Jay settles into the driver's side. "Don't you have to work the crime scene?"

"I'm not interested in what's inside that house. I'm interested in what's not." I dial Lucas on speakerphone, and it goes straight to voicemail. Again. Next, I dial Tic Tac, and he answers on the first ring.

"Let me guess. You need stuff."

"Lots of stuff, but let's start with where the hell is Lucas?"

"Ditto. His phone tracks to his house. I'm one person with about one hundred time-sensitive items I should be researching."

And he's smart enough to know he can't use agency resources when there are government targets, not when we don't know who's involved. "Any leads on Elsa?"

"All I can tell you is she had twenty recorded sniper kills in the military. That's a lot. And her mother had a stroke and died about six months before her father's suicide."

"She's bitter and skilled."

"Which is why I need help to make traction and get you answers."

"I get it," I say. "I'm going to find Lucas."

Like a good little soldier, Jay cranks the SUV and sets us in motion.

"You need to focus all energy on finding Elsa,"

"Surely she'll come to you. Her brother was murdered."

I find myself flip-flopping like a dirty politician who doesn't have his own mind over who killed Mark Walker—Ghost or his sister. It's utterly frustrating. I don't flip-flop. I hate flip-flopping. Maybe because my father is so good at it.

Nevertheless, I do a mental replay of the possibilities again. Elsa could have been at odds with Mark over the revenge killings, and when he threatened to turn her in, she killed him. But as the Ken doll ME pointed out, Mark's body was posed. Elsa would not pose the body. Ghost would, as a taunt.

I'm back to Ghost did it for about the fourth time.

I'm done with that question.

That decided, I think back to my chat with Ghost, to what he said about finding Elsa. *She thinks she's hiding*, he'd said.

He's smart. She's killing for revenge, and revenge is an emotion. He's studied her. He believes he knows what that emotion will drive in her, what she will do next. Maybe he doesn't think he knows. He knows. Maybe he taunted her. Maybe he's waiting for her right here.

"Lilah?"

Tic Tac draws me back to the present, and I don't resist. I'm doing nothing but speculating, and that amounts to chasing my own tail like a puppy Ghost has on a leash. Only he's chasing me, and I can use that to my advantage.

"Lilah?"

Apparently, I'm still ignoring Tic Tac. I need to be in Purgatory, but I can't afford the time right now. "Where's Ellis?" I ask. "He's not answering his phone."

"He pings in Maryland, and," he grunts and says, "Jack, what are you doing? No. Give me that phone."

The next thing I know, Jack is on the line. "I still say going to Maryland feels like a lame move on Ellis' part. Elsa's too smart to take her phone with her to kill a government official, and how can the Director of Homeland Security not think of that?"

"I'm still here," Tic Tac says, letting me know we're on speakerphone on his end too, now, but I'm thinking about what Jack just said.

Why indeed, I think. What does Ellis know that we don't know? *Too much*, I think.

"It's like something the cop does in a B horror flick," Jack continues. "You know everyone is going to die because he's the idiot that's supposed to be saving them."

But who is Ellis saving, besides himself? If he wasn't pinging in Maryland, I'd think he was on the run. Does he think he knows the next target? I pull the list of committee members from my pocket that Ellis gave me. Has he warned them all they're in danger?

Jack is talking, talking, talking, presently about Dexter. "The brilliant thing about Dexter is that he was a serial killer in plain sight. He seemed normal, almost too normal, and Elsa's essentially a—"

"Stop talking, Jack. Tic Tac?"

"I'm here."

"I'm texting you a list of everyone on the committee that killed Clyde's contract, thus will be a target for Elsa. Find out where each one is now. And get me phone numbers for every one of them. And," I sigh, "I can't believe I'm saying this, but get me a line to the president."

"I—you—*the president*?"

"That's right. Get me a line to the president."

He's silent.

"*Tic Tac.*"

"Okay. On it. I'm putting you on hold."

At this point, we've pulled into the driveway of Lucas' place, and Jay halts in front of the door. I motion for him to get out and then text the list to Tic Tac that I should have given him before now. It's a full five minutes later when Tic Tac comes back on the line. "He'll call you back."

"Said every powerful man avoiding a woman who wants to bust his balls," I mumble, and then firmer, "Work on the list."

"The VP is on the list?"

"Yes, the VP is on the list. Now you know why I want to talk to the president."

"That's not why. You don't trust Ellis."

"When have you known me to trust anyone?" I don't give him a chance to reply. I hang up. I didn't trust Murphy. I sure as fuck don't trust Ellis, perhaps to the extreme. He just got to Maryland. He can't answer his phone while raiding Elsa's place, which is apparently where assassins for the government get trained.

I should at least give him the bad girlfriend. I dial Ellis and get thrown into voicemail again. I try three more times. Finally, I text him: *Call me before I do something crazy. There are ideas in my head. That's never a good thing.*

I don't wait for a reply. I'm perfectly capable of texting and yelling at Lucas all at once. I'm a good multitasker. I exit the truck, and Jay is standing by the front door.

I climb the steps to meet him. "Did you ring the bell?"

"Ten times while freezing my ass off waiting on you. Nothing."

I pat his arm. "Poor cold baby. Fuck the police academy. You need a cushy office job with a warm heater, a pretty receptionist to flirt with, and bad grocery store cake for birthday parties."

With that, I offer him my back and hurry down the stairs. Apparently, Jay, too, can multitask, as he groans a complaint and follows me at the same time.

I hike it right and round the house and then come around by the pool, with Jay tight on my heels. I'd teach him a lesson about safe distances by stopping and letting him crash into me, but there's no time for tears and hard-earned lessons. I need Lucas to get to work. He can find a needle in a haystack if it starts with a keyboard, and Elsa and her next victim are that needle.

Once I'm at the sliding glass door, I don't bother to knock. If it didn't work on the front door, it's not going to work on the back. Besides, I don't want to lose the chance to throw ice water on him to wake him up. Lucas never locks the back of the house, and the door slides open easily.

I shove the curtain back and listen for any sound, unease niggling at my belly. I lift a hand, telling Jay to stay back. My hand settles on my firearm, and I ease through the archway to find a couple empty pizza boxes and whiskey bottles. Obviously, Tic Tac wasn't wrong. Lucas is drinking again, but the leap of my pulse is confirmation that that is not all that's going on here.

I draw my weapon and ease to the right to peek into the bedroom, then step inside, find the bed unmade, clothes on the floor, and the master bath messy as fuck, but all clear. Once I'm back in the living area, there's a popping sound, like a beer can opening, that draws my attention toward the kitchen. I hurry that direction and round the corner.

Lucas is sitting at the kitchen table, a beer in hand and looking like a homeless person, not a beach bum, with his hair matted and standing on end, but he's not alone.

There's a fifty-something man sitting across from him, his hands in front of him—his *roped* hands in front of him. And I know who this is. I met him at one of my father's events. He's Pocher's head of security, who was somehow dumb enough to get captured by my dumbass drunk cousin.

"What is this, Lucas?"

"If anyone knows the details of our parents dying in that plane that night, this bastard does."

CHAPTER TWELVE

The definition of stupid used to be Andrew. Now it's Lucas. He officially won the top spot. If I opened the now long-obsolete dictionary, I bet there's a picture of him in a diaper subtitled "stupid was born." I holster my weapon, walk over to Lucas, and take his gun from him. He gives a blustery objection while the head of security, whom I'll call dumbass number two, as Lucas gets the dumbass number one spot, laughs.

"Really?" I challenge incredulously. "You're laughing at him? The drunk guy who just let me take his gun?"

"He wasn't drunk when he kidnapped me."

I snort. "You did see how easily I took his gun, right?"

"He's drunk."

"If you doubt me, I can leave you tied up until he's sober and give him the gun back. I'm confident I can save you again."

He's a big, fit guy with red hair, and when he grits his teeth, the red blush of anger overtakes his plentiful freckles. "If I cared what happened to Pocher, I'd tell him to fire you." He opens his mouth to speak, and I point the gun at him. "Silence."

He draws in a breath, his chin bobbing with agreement. My attention returns to Lucas, who's presently tipping back a bottle. I set the gun in my hand on a counter and knock the booze from his hand. "Stop it. Stop drinking. You're going to rehab, you fool."

"I don't want to go to rehab. I want answers."

"Then try being sober enough to be smart about getting them."

He pushes to his feet and turns to face me. "I'm not that drunk," he says as he sways slightly.

"I got up too fast," he groans.

"*I got up too fast,*" I mock. "Of course, you did. And that ruddy tone to your skin is just a sunburn. If you're not drunk, you can do your job." His computer is sitting at the end of the table, and I open it. "Sit and find Elsa Walker. Her phone is in Maryland, but I know she is not. And if you can't find her, I need to make a good guess on her next victim based on the target list."

"He knows, Lilah. He knows about our parents."

I glance over at the man. "What's your name?"

"Paul."

"Okay, *Paul*. When did you go to work for Pocher?"

"Three years ago this Christmas."

I eye Lucas. "Okay, my dumbass cousin. He wasn't with Pocher when it happened."

"He *knows*."

"Even if he does, he wouldn't tell you. He'd end up dead."

"I'll kill him if he doesn't," he bites out, his fingers curled into his palms. "I will."

He's lost it, and I'm starting to think there's more than booze involved. "Sit down and hack."

"I thought I was your dumbass cousin?"

"What's so sad, Lucas, is you're the smartest dumbass I've ever known. Stop being a girl. You don't get a period. You don't have the excuse of raging hormones, but I do. And my hormones are powerful bitches. They want me to hurt you right now. *Sit down* and hack. It's your *job*."

"I'm beginning to think you don't have ovaries. You're such a bitch."

"Thank you." I eye Jay where he hovers at the entryway. "Tell Enrique that Paul needs a ride home."

He pales again. It's a mighty trick. The next thing I know, he'll be in Docker shorts playing tennis. "What?" I press.

"He's with Kane."

"That's his problem, not mine. Tell him I need him at Lucas' house."

He gives a sharp nod and backs out of the doorway. "Paul," I say, as he earned my attention again. "I'm not going to kill you. It's tempting. It really is, but it's messy, and I don't have time for messy. We both know you can't tell Pocher you were stupid enough to get kidnapped without looking incompetent; therefore, I won't kill you." I pull my phone out and shoot a photo of him, the rope around his hands.

I check out my work and then turn it around to show him. His mouth is open. If he had a little drool, it would be a perfect little bitch shot. "Pocher should be impressed, don't you think?" I query, all sticky sweet. "That's a good knot he worked around your wrists, too." I flick a look at Lucas. "Impressive."

"I've been practicing," he mumbles.

It's a confession that tells me he's been off the deep end and drowning longer than I know. "We'll talk about that statement later."

I return my attention to Paul. "I'll keep the photo for my personal album, unless you give me a reason to use it otherwise."

"I'm supposed to be on duty. I'm going to have to explain where I was."

"That's a problem for you to figure out. Or we can call Pocher together, if you'd rather. I'll tell him I ran a test on his security before election night on Tuesday after the massive rally failure. Spoiler. You failed the test."

"I'll keep my mouth shut," he grumbles, and with that win, I glare at Lucas, who's still standing and presently staring at Paul. "Lucas," I snap, pointing at the chair. "Sit. Hack."

Enrique appears in the doorway. "What the fuck, Lilah?"

"Oh, relax. You're not burying him, Enrique, though Lucas is making me want to cut him." I glower at him again. "Sit down, Lucas." This time he sits.

My attention returns to Enrique. "Just take him back to Pocher, will you?"

"Who is he?"

"Pocher's head of security," Paul states.

Enrique's gaze shoots to Lucas. "You did this?"

"I'm a capable person."

"Spoken with a slur a half bottle deep," I comment dryly, motioning to the evidence on the table. "Which is why you have to go to rehab—after you find Elsa Walker."

Paul stiffens. "What about Elsa Walker?"

My gaze rockets to his. "You know her?"

"She and her brother attended a campaign event recently and had VIP backstage passes. I believe Mark donated money to the campaign."

Okay, I think. This is unexpected when perhaps it shouldn't have been. Pocher, and now my father, it seems, are into just about everything. And since there's no such thing as a coincidence, I'd assume this time is no exception.

"Change of plans," I announce. "I'm coming along for the ride to Pocher's place."

If Pocher's involved, I know exactly how to get him to talk.

CHAPTER THIRTEEN

"I hate to burst your bubble," Paul says, but he doesn't sound like he hates it at all. "I'm not here with Pocher. With the election four days away, he's not leaving your father's side in the city." He lifts a chin at Lucas. "He snatched me when I arrived to pick up important documents Pocher needed. I never made it past the airport."

The damn election.

Wait.

The election.

I pull the list from my pocket and show it to Paul. "How many of those people are on the guest list?"

He eyes me. "Why?"

"Because they're about to die at the hands of a skilled assassin, and so are you if I leave you with Lucas. Not by a skilled assassin, but he'll eventually hit you if I give him the gun back. Answer the question."

"Three from memory. There might be more."

"Call and find out."

"Lucas has my phone."

Lucas grunts and slides it across the table, right between Paul's tied hands. Paul punches a button on the phone and manages to shove it to his ear. "Dave," he greets, and after a silence, he adds, "My chopper had mechanical issues. I'm still in the Hamptons. I need you to check the invitation list for election night."

I listen to him read off the names and argue with Dave a minute before he disconnects. "Just the three I mentioned. I need to tell my team there's a security challenge."

"If you think it's a smart decision to go around me, then you go around me, Paul." My lips curve. "I think I might enjoy how that turns out."

I ignore him and hand the list to Lucas. "She'll go after the ones who won't be at the event. Find those three." I don't wait for his confirmation and eye Enrique. "He needs a ride home that's not with us. Make it happen."

Enrique rounds the table and orders Paul to his feet while Jay hovers. "I won't say anything," he says to me, "for now. I can't allow the event to go down without extra security."

"Because you want to keep Pocher and my father safe?"

"Yes."

"That tells me all I need to know about you, Paul." I wave Enrique on and then tell Jay, "Go with him."

"But—"

"Don't argue. Go. With. Him."

His lips curl over his teeth like a dog about to bark, and he backs out of the room. I sit down across from Lucas. "What is wrong with you?"

"What is wrong with *you*, Lilah?" he demands, and he's a lot more sober than I'd believed. His voice is steady, his anger precise and cutting. "You're an FBI agent, and you haven't done shit to get justice for my father or your mother. We know they were murdered now. That changes everything."

"Maybe I should go kidnap everyone, kill them, and have Kane bury the bodies. Is that what you want from me?"

"You bet your ass I do, but I'd settle for you doing anything, Lilah. Your fucking brother is going to work for your father, which means Pocher. One or both of them killed my father and your mother."

"He's trying to help by getting on the inside."

"They'll corrupt him. That's what that is. And how much money did they offer him?"

"He doesn't need money any more than I need money. Mom left us both a small fortune."

"Power is like a beautiful blonde with a great body and huge boobs on display while she offers to get on her knees. Do you really think your brother is strong enough to turn that down?"

"He's one of the best men we both know, Lucas. Revenge is a dangerous high that will end up getting you killed."

"And you don't want it?"

"I want more. Everything Pocher and my father do relates to the Society. I want the real leader, the one calling the shots. That's not Pocher. It's not my father, but my father is the way inside to get at that person. And as for this case I'm working, Murphy knew a lot of things he can't tell me now, but the victims on the hit list Elsa Walker intends to kill might. They can't tell us if they're dead, too. We need to stop Elsa from killing them."

"I assume since you're going to visit Pocher's place, you think Pocher can help with that?"

"He only helps when I leave him no choice, which is my intent." I push to my feet. "Elsa's phone—"

"Is in Maryland, but she is not."

"Exactly. Have Tic Tac send you the hit list and find a way to figure out who is next. Or just find her." I start to move and hesitate. "Find Director Ellis. He won't return my calls. He's in Maryland looking for her, but it feels off."

"You think he's dead or dirty?"

"Maybe both if he found Elsa. Text or call me with updates. And call Tic Tac. He's afraid to let anyone but you help him considering the high-level government officials involved."

"You mean he's afraid to break the rules he needs to break to give you what you want."

"We both know Tic Tac is the light to your darkness."

"And what are you?"

"A bitch who will cut you if you don't get me what I want."

"You know the worst part of you saying that to your loving cousin? I believe you."

"My *loving cousin*." I snort. "Whatever." I tilt my head and study him. "You aren't drunk."

"Nope."

"Why play drunk?"

"You took my gun. I needed a reason to be that stupid."

I almost laugh. *Almost.* Right now, it's me against Ghost, and he's a worthy enough opponent, but arrogant to a flaw. He thinks he's the smartest killer I've ever faced.

He's wrong. That was Roger, my mentor and The Umbrella Man. And now he's dead.

CHAPTER FOURTEEN

Kane believes Lucas wants to get into my pants; therefore, I expect Kane to be waiting on me outside while fantasizing about giving Lucas a slow, painful death.

Kane hates Lucas.

The whole "cousin" thing when we aren't blood-related just infuriates him. And regardless of why I called for him now, knowing Kane, in his mind, he sees me heading straight from a battle with him to Lucas' house—*to Lucas*—as the deepest cut I could have delivered, which is absolute bullshit. And for Lucas' safety, it's a premise I need to snuff like a bad habit.

Or Pocher.

Yes, let's snuff Pocher. What a birthday gift that would be!

I exit Lucas' house to find the SUV parked at the bottom of the stairs with Kit, one of Kane's most trusted men, leaning on the door. He offers me a mini salute as Kane pushes off the wall next to me and shows himself, predator waiting on prey, only I'm never prey, and he knows it. Ever. But I hope like hell Ghost makes the mistake of believing otherwise. I also wonder how much longer Kane's jealousy and agitation would have allowed him to wait outside for me. Not much longer, I suspect, considering he made it this far.

I face off with Kane, toe-to-toe, as he towers over me. To most, Kane is as good-looking as he is intimidating, even terrifying. He doesn't have that advantage with me, and he knows it. A big man has never intimidated me. In fact, it places me in the sweet pocket to cause damage to the family jewels, though in Kane's case, I wouldn't go that far. A wife doesn't need such violence. She has her ways.

"You know he has cameras with audio?" I ask, a warning to watch what he says. I might not be happy with him, nor do I agree with him on Lucas and his motives, but some part of me does not want Lucas knowing things that might hurt Kane. I should probably analyze that feeling at some point that is not now.

"Of course I know, bella," he purrs, a mix of steel and acid beneath the precisely spoken words. "I *want him* to know that I'm here. Why are *you* here?"

I don't bother to point out his possessiveness. A statement of fact we both already understand serves no purpose. "I'm not going to be for long," I assure him. "We need to talk. *In private.*"

"I tried that, and you walked away."

"Not about your shitty decisions under my radar. I had a visitor tonight. You can guess who."

"I heard," he murmurs, his voice as sharp as a fresh blade. "Is he dead?"

"Assuming as much is a stretch and a compliment that will get you nowhere, Kane. You're in deep shit with me."

"You need to step back and see what I did for what it is. I made sure my father can't control us. We control him."

"They control us," I say in obvious reference to the mob.

"You're underestimating both of us if you think that's true. No one can control us now, not even Ghost."

Ghost is one of the main reasons I taunted the bear, aka Kane, into following Enrique over here. He knows Ghost, probably better than even I know he knows him. But we've said too much where we stand, and as if he's in the same headspace, Kane motions toward the SUV where Kit has made himself scarce.

We rotate together, in tune with one another even when at odds, and for a moment, just a moment, I like how that feels. And that like, that love, softens my anger without ending it. He believes he took control. I'm not sure how the mob lends itself to that premise, and right now, it's me who needs to be in control.

Not Elsa. And sure as fuck not Ghost. Right now, that's exactly what feels like is happening. He's in control. I wonder if Elsa has figured that out yet. I'd call her and make sure she does, but she doesn't have her phone with her.

We reach the SUV, and again, Kane and I rotate to face each other. He steps closer. "Damn it, woman, you're going to be the death of me."

"That's exactly right," I assure him, even as his hand comes down on my face and his mouth crashes over mine. His lips are warm, a stark contrast to the cold night air and the death that suffocates me in its finality.

I don't resist him. I'm not that selfless, I'm just not. I will take the last donut. I will eat the whole pie. I will allow Kane to make me moan. I'm angry with him, I might as well enjoy him while I allow him to live. Besides, you learn a lot about a man in how he kisses you.

For instance, Kane tastes of whiskey and worry, and some salty something that is as addictive as this man needing me as much as he does. There was a time when I wouldn't have admitted I want this from him, even crave this from him, and this is exactly why. It distracts me. It's dangerous, and this has gone too far.

I shove away from him.

"Stop kissing me like I almost died or you're about to." I point up at him. I seem to be a pointer today. It must be my way of not hitting everyone, especially him. "You need to stop a lot of things right now."

"All right," he states, anger ripping a note in his words. "What the hell was Ghost doing here?"

"That's complicated."

"I'm not exactly a simple man, bella, in case you didn't notice."

No, I think. He is not, but he sure as fuck makes burying a body as simple. The question is, why doesn't Ghost know that, and was tonight even about me? Was Ghost challenging Kane? And if so, why?

CHAPTER FIFTEEN

If you ever wondered what it's like to stand at the base of a volcano about to erupt, live vicariously through me now. I dare you.

Kane stares at me, and I swear I can see the fires of Hell glow in the depths of his otherwise brown eyes. Ghost has crossed a line with him, and I can't believe Ghost is dumb enough to do such a thing. He had to have known he was taunting a bull; but then, Ghost planned to kill me. Did he plan to kill Kane, too?

Taunt him?

What is really going on here?

Nothing good, and there really isn't any way around telling Kane the truth, the whole truth, and nothing but the truth, no matter what it ignites in him.

I steel myself and get right to the worst of it. "Ghost called me from a burner phone."

"Ghost called you?" Kane's voice is low, steady, but there is the promise of death in those words. "How the fuck does he even have your number?"

"He clearly has his own version of Tic Tac."

"Why? What did he want?"

"We need to backtrack a minute for you to have context."

"What fucking context, Lilah?"

Okay, then. He's prickly times ten fucking thousand. "There was a committee that denied Clyde Walker a contract for personal gains. He killed himself, at least officially per the records. We believe his grown kids tried to hire a hitman to take out the committee members, which included Murphy, as a point of interest, and the vice president. No one would take the job; therefore, the daughter, who's a sniper, is doing the job herself."

"And Ghost wants her dead, because she's the one who took the number one assassin rank." He says it as a matter of fact. This isn't my first encounter with Ghost, and he's made his mission quite clear. Only I'm not sure what he says is what he does anymore.

"That still doesn't tell me why he called you," Kane adds, drawing me back into the moment.

"I was notified that Mark Walker was dead. At that point, I didn't know if his sister had turned on him, if someone on the committee went after them, or what. That is until I was at the airport preparing to fly out when my phone rang with an unknown number. I'm sure you can guess it was Ghost. His intent was to taunt me because he was at the crime scene and I was not."

"He killed Mark."

"I wasn't sure at first, but for a variety of reasons, I am now. So yes. He killed him. I don't have motive locked down. Perhaps to lure Elsa to him, since she's off the grid. Her phone has been parked in Maryland, unmoving for days. Which, sidenote: Ellis rushed off to Maryland to find her, despite her ping saying she's not with her phone."

"Dirty?"

"Or scared and hiding. I'm not sure. I'm questioning what I really know about anything right now."

"Which is a good reason to get back to Ghost."

"Right. Ghost. Apparently, he's been watching me. He wanted me to bring him strawberry pie. I figured a pie requires a knife, so I took him a pie."

Kane pinches the bridge of his nose and mutters in Spanish before his hands land on his hips. "Go on."

"I got there to find Mark was splayed across the piano, posed when the other victims were not. One might assume it's to agitate Elsa, but I don't like to assume. I'll call it a hypothesis I'm trying to prove. He had plates and silverware waiting. Long story short, neither of us planned on the other leaving alive, but there were word games."

His brows shoot up. "Word games?"

"Yes. Word games, during which I might have mentioned my love of blades and killing come from my first kill. The man my father sent to kill me."

"And you let him live after you told him that?"

"I didn't plan to," I bristle. "He decided he would give me a gift and kill my father as soon as he has his number one status back. In other words, after he kills Elsa. He no sooner stated this then the lights went out and he was gone."

I've barely finished my explanation, and he's opening the back of the SUV, capturing my hand and dragging me forward. "Get inside."

I rotate to find myself pinned between the vehicle and my man. "I have a murder to investigate."

"You do not know Ghost like I know Ghost. Get in the fucking car, Lilah."

I try to choose my battles smartly, and this is not one I'm going to win, so why fight it? I get in the fucking car.

CHAPTER SIXTEEN

Kit scrambles from a slouch position behind the wheel as Kane pulls the door shut and barks out an order his direction. "Have our house searched. We'll wait to enter. No. Scratch that. We're going to the diner to eat pie while we wait." Kane shoots me a sideways stare. "And I dare Ghost to come anywhere near us."

"If he wanted me dead," I say as Kane pulls the door shut behind us, "*he'd* be dead."

The look he gives me could cut through steel, and his tone isn't one bit gentler as he assumes the inevitable. "You saw his face again?"

I see no reason to deny the truth. "I don't think I ever saw it clearly until tonight. I thought I did, but that sketch I had done looks nothing like him. He told me he changes his appearance and has certain personas for certain people. My sketch looked like the Ghost you know, right?"

"Yes. It did."

"He didn't look the same, Kane. I really think he showed me the real him. He was that arrogant and certain he'd kill me, not the opposite way around. I need to get him sketched fast, while he's fresh in my mind."

"I'll get you someone I trust." He eyes Kit in the mirror.

"On it," Kit says, and he's already pulling us out of the driveway.

Deflecting the topic of the implications of me seeing Ghost's face, I focus on the business at hand. "I don't have time for the diner. I need to be in Purgatory. We can wait in the car for them to clear the house, which isn't necessary. Ghost has other people on his mind, at least for now."

"He has you on his mind," Kane snaps. "And I don't like it. We're going for pie. If he's following us, I'm sending him a message. He doesn't eat pie with you. I do."

"Do you even know how crazy that sounds? What does that even mean?"

"He'll know what it means."

"Okay," I say, though it's not okay. We're not okay, at least not right now. So much so that when my phone buzzes with back-to-back text messages, I act out of character. I curl my fingers into my palms to stop myself from reaching for it. I'm quite aware of the fact that Kane's going to erupt if I present him that kind of distraction from me right now.

As if proving my point, he presses his elbows on his knees and lowers his chin. "Damn it, Lilah," he mutters under his breath as if I'm not right here, ready for whatever the "damn it" indicates is coming at us.

I sigh in utter frustration.

He straightens and rounds on me. "Do not sigh like that at me. He's not like anyone you have faced. Not even the Umbrella Man, Lilah. Ghost *is* a ghost. I can't just go kill him before he kills us. And yet, that is exactly what has to happen."

"He wants Elsa. We find her, we find him."

"You *think,* which is assuming, and that's not like you. And that's the exact fuckup that's going to get you killed. Nothing with Ghost is what it seems. For all you know, killing Mark wasn't about Elsa at all. It was about you."

"Or you. What's between you and Ghost, Kane?"

He stares at me for several heavy beats and then shifts gears. "Take us home, Kit." In other words, there is much to say, and none of it in public.

Alright then.

He and Ghost have more of a history than I ever considered. What is it, and why hasn't Kane told me about it before now? More secrets, obviously, but is something I simply had no need up to this point of knowing really a problem? I suspect there are many things I'm in the dark about where his past comes into play, and I have to be careful about a demand to know all that reverts rather than faces forward. I'm a reasonable person, no matter who lies otherwise.

We don't speak the remainder of the short ride, and by the time we're at the house, my phone has gone off a dozen times that I've been forced to ignore. I've also replayed my interactions with Ghost with a perspective that places him at the bottom of my priority list. I'm antsy, ready to get out of this vehicle and inside Purgatory.

We arrive at our house to find my brother already past the gate and at the front door, no doubt compliments of his badge and Kane's men, who seem to be present in excess. Wonderful. It's a party, and everyone is looking for all the devious ways Ghost could kill us when he chose not to even try with me.

It's illogical, but here we are. Living the good life.

The minute the SUV halts, I reach for the door, and Kane reaches for me, his hand coming down firmly on my arm. "Wait, Lilah," he bites out.

I've had about enough of his alpha, arrogant, bossy self right now, and I face off with him, ready for battle. "I'm not leaving my brother to search our house. I don't even want him to know you're worried, Kane. He'll lose his shit and freak the fuck out. As if either of us can take that kind of energy right now."

Kit exits the vehicle and slams the door shut behind him.

Kane shockingly clenches his teeth and releases me without so much as a grunt. I guess the idea of dealing with my brother when he's in overload was all he needed to reconsider getting any further into this with me until my brother is gone. I get it. Andrew's Jay on steroids, and that's a circus at best, performed by one person who I can't believe came from the same womb as me at times.

I shove open the door and step outside, luckily on the opposite side of the vehicle from the house and out of view. With that shelter in place, I don't rush away, waiting on one last word with my dear, loving, oh-so-reasonable husband. Husband dearest joins me with an attitude with so much bite I'm surprised he doesn't grow fangs, but I approve. "Keep that up," I encourage.

His scowl deepens, proving the impossible possible, and I swear it's carved from the bowels of Hell by the devil himself. "Keep what up?"

77

"Your attitude is a good way to get rid of my brother, and hallelujah for it. Especially since I know what he wants."

"Which is what?"

"For us to decide if we're going to warn my father about Ghost vowing to kill him or just let Ghost kill him."

"What do you want, bella?" His voice has softened, a rasp in his tone, a hint of accent lacing the endearment.

"I don't need Ghost to do my dirty work. When the time comes, I'll happily kill him myself. Any objections?"

"No. I'll happily bury that body, bella. You just name the time and place."

"I like that plan, but just as a reminder, I'll probably make it highly emotional, poorly timed, and difficult to hide. Ghost won't be as complicated. You won't have to bury him or hide him." I shove his chest. "Stop doubting me, you asshole." With that, I start to turn away.

Kane pulls me back to him, his arm wrapping my waist. "We have much to discuss, Lilah."

"Oh, we do indeed. You seem to forget just how much you have to answer for." I push away from him and start walking, leaving him behind, but not for long.

There's a war brewing between me and my husband that's at present positively volcanic. I'd like to stave off the eruption until after my brother leaves, but whatever. If it has to be sooner, so be it.

CHAPTER SEVENTEEN

My brother is actually an amazing human being who has a knack for finding the stupid spot in the line, which, of course, makes him look *stupid* when he's not. And what's a sister for if not to tell him just that? Okay, I normally don't say the good parts or admit he's not stupid. I mean, I'm his sister. If not for me, his ego might be the size of my father's, and that would not be acceptable.

And when you look at it that way, I've done him and the world a service by keeping him in line. I've certainly done his future wife a service, which reminds me...

I join him on the porch. "You still fucking Kane's ex-bimbo?"

Raz, or Taz, or whatever his name is, is standing by the door behind Andrew and chokes on laughter. Andrew doesn't notice, probably because he's too busy scowling at me. "Really, Lilah?"

"Really, Andrew, and I take that as a yes. Are you getting regular medical screenings? Also, why don't we hold a birthday party, and you can bring her? It'll be fun."

"Can we focus on the problems at hand?"

"She is a problem, Andrew. Wait and see."

"*Lilah?*"

"What do you want to talk about, big brother? Mark is dead. Elsa and Ghost are missing. I'm going to Purgatory to work on finding them."

"Dad. I want to talk about Dad."

"Ghost doesn't care about Dad right now. He cares about Elsa."

Kane joins us on the porch, and there's a subtle stiffening of Andrew's spine that tells me he's still not okay with my husband.

"Andrew," Kane greets.

"If you're afraid of him, Andrew," I say, "why are you at his home?"

79

Andrew bristles. "Do you wake up and take a bitch pill?" He eyes Kane. "Can you not give her the damn pill?"

Kane laughs low and deep, failing miserably at remaining the grumpy, scary dude who's supposed to scare off my brother. "She's a piece of work today," he claims, and he's right. He better remember it, too, because he's pushing his luck with me. The mob? Really? "I need a drink," Kane says, and lifting a chin at my brother, adds, "You need a drink, Andrew?"

"Aren't they clearing the house?"

"They did a wide sweep," Kane confirms. "They can work the rest around us." He sidesteps Andrew and saunters toward the door, disappearing inside with Kit and then Raz on his heels.

The minute we're alone, my brother is back at it. "Should we be warning Dad right now?"

"Not yet."

"Should we talk to Kane about it?"

"I already talked to Kane about it."

"And he said?"

"So now you've officially gone from wanting to put Kane in jail to hanging by a thread for his opinion? I should have taken a photo of the fear in your eyes when he joined us."

"I'm not afraid of Kane. And once you bury a body with a man, you trust him with the next one."

And the body they buried was for me. Only I don't feel one little bit guilty over it, either. It was Roger after all, and Roger was a serial killer, which reminds me of what the ME said about Mark's murder. An assassin is not a serial killer. He's hired to kill for a monetary reward. That's a different beast. Even killing Mark was simply about protecting his status, which translates to his income.

"Lilah?"

At Andrew's prodding, I snap back into the moment. "You know if Dad dies, you'll need a job. Maybe you shouldn't give yours away so fast." He opens his mouth to speak, and I stop him with a raised hand. "I'm not sure Ghost intends to kill him at all."

"Then why say it?"

"It's a distraction. Go work the case. Who's taking over for you, and why wasn't that person present tonight?"

"Chief Taylor, coming in from Nassau County. He's been here part-time. He starts full time Monday, but he's on his way down now." His phone buzzes with a text. "I need to get back to the crime scene. There's press gathering around the gate. I need to decide if I'm talking to them."

"We need Elsa to come to us. We need her distracted from her next hit. And I need her and Ghost in one place to end them. Talk to the press."

"You want in on it?"

"Nope. I don't want Elsa to be intimidated by my badge. You get some men to watch the place. I'll have Kane get them backup." He nods and heads down the stairs, pausing at the bottom and glancing back at me. "You really want a party?"

"Like I want a hole in my head." I turn and head for the door.

He calls after me, "Okay, a party it is."

I roll my eyes and offer him my back, making my way to the door. I know him. He's going to throw me a party, and I'm going to have to kick his ass. As for how to celebrate my birthday—really celebrate—I'll kick back, relax with a lemon drop martini, and watch Andrew dig a grave. I just haven't decided who will go in it yet. Maybe he should dig two or three to be safe.

CHAPTER EIGHTEEN

My phone rings as I reach for the door to the house.

I always find people brave enough to actually call me interesting creatures destined to either earn my respect or wrath. Since I have God knows how many murders at this point to solve, I decide now's a good time to reward their bravery. Caller ID shows an "unknown" number, which lends to a good chance this is either the president or Ghost. I'd prefer the latter, as ending Ghost means no more calls from the president.

At least, I sure as fuck hope it means that.

"Agent Mendez," I answer, claiming Mendez over Love, considering my husband has apparently made my gangster status official.

"Special Agent Love-Mendez."

"Mr. President," I greet, because I can be respectful. I just don't respect a whole lot of people. The leader of the free world gets it, though, at least until I find out he's a bigger gangster than Kane.

"I assume we have a problem," he prods.

"Have you talked to Director Ellis?"

"I have not. Should I have?"

"He's radio silent," I explain. "I assume this line is clear?"

"It is."

It is oh so clear and yet not clear at all, and I press, "Is it recorded, or is anyone listening?"

"No to both."

He sounds certain even if I am not. But he knows he has two dead directors. I have to give him the benefit of the doubt and assume if he can run a country, he can find a private line to make a phone call. "We have a hit list that may match the members of a committee Ellis himself was on," I state. "I believe the vice president was a member as well. I'd lock him down until I notify you otherwise."

There are three silent beats, and then, "That's disconcerting. Have we lost Ellis?"

"I don't like to assume, Mr. President. Ellis gave me the committee list. He's missing. I think we're both intelligent enough to know that leaves a lot of room for assumption but no proof."

"What *do* we know?"

"Not enough, and when high-level officials are targets, I'm not comfortable saying more. I don't want my target warned I'm on my way."

"Then you have a target?"

"More than one."

He's silent another few beats. "You don't trust Ellis." It's not a question, and he doesn't wait for an answer nor ask an explanation. "What about Adams?"

"Forgive me, Mr. President, but I don't even trust you. You are, after all, the number one politician in the world. And you know what they say about politicians? The only time he tells the truth is when he calls another politician a liar."

He chuckles. "I like you, agent. My mother-in-law would like you as well. That's her favorite joke."

"Is it a joke?"

He's back to chuckling. "You really don't give two fucks that I'm the president, and it's a ray of sunshine in a city of hogwash."

"Hogwash again?"

"I speak with delicate words but mark my words, when I go to battle, I fight bloody and fiercely. What else, agent?"

"The VP would be smart to hire private security."

"Done. Keep in contact."

"Done."

He disconnects.

I dial Ellis again, and when I land in voicemail, I curse. If anyone knows Murphy and what Murphy was up to, it was Ellis. I really don't want him to be dirty. Or dead.

My phone rings, and I glance down to find Adams' number. Huh. Right after I talk to the president. What are the odds? And yet, I'm not sure the president had time to call him. Unless he was with the president? Irritated by the games I seem to be forced to play, I answer with, "Who's this?"

"You know who this is, Special Agent Mendez."

"No. No, I really don't. Because the acting director of the FBI would be here right now, helping catch the person killing off directors, and since you are not, you must be an imposter. Or the acting director with something to gain."

"Keep it coming, agent. I expect nothing less from you. I'm on my way to Maryland."

Now he has my attention. "Why Maryland?"

"Ellis called me and said if he didn't contact me in twelve hours, he's dead, and I should go get his body. He's not answering. I trust you have things under control there, because I was in depositions today for a case that went south on Murphy's watch. I'll be back in court on Monday, unless Ellis went and got himself killed. Is there anything I need to know, aside from the fact that Elsa Walker is a sniper?"

Clearly Ellis did talk to him. I'm just not sure if it was in the context of a cover-up or solving the case. "I'd have to trust you to tell you what you need to know, and right now, I do not."

He grunts. "All right, then. Here's to hoping you aren't picking up me and Ellis in body bags." He disconnects.

I stand there and consider my phone calls and decide I really can't trust any of them. Which is, as the president would say, a bunch of hogwash.

CHAPTER NINETEEN

I walk into the kitchen to find Kane standing with Kit and Raz, their voices low, words unintelligible, and, of course, there's not a glass of liquor in sight. Kane didn't want a drink. He wanted out of the conversation with Andrew.

In the meantime, my pie sits between the three men, but the price of conversation I'll have to pay to get it and a fork just isn't worth it. I'm kind of tired of that damn pie anyway, at least tonight.

"Hello, boys," I say. All eyes lift to me in the doorway, and now that I have their attention, I add, "I'm done with Enrique. If he shows up on my team one more time, I'll shoot him. That's it. Go back to whispering things you don't want me to hear, but I'll find out anyway."

I walk away, leaving them behind in every sense possible. I have messages I have not even looked at, and not one, but three murders to solve. I head toward our lower-level bedroom that was once upstairs, but Kane surprised me a month back with a remodel. Now our primary is not only on the lower level, but he had a proper loft version of Purgatory, just like I had in my mother's place, created.

We still haven't done anything with the property that holds the charred remains of my memories, now ash beneath the structure, but I've refused to let go of the heart bleeding in the rubble. In fact, I've been leaning toward something wonderful, like a museum celebrating her life that also saves puppies. It might seem like a weird combination to some, but if they knew my mother and how earnestly she approached helping animals in need, they'd understand.

There's a twist of emotion in my belly that few things create in me but this.

Her.

Her death.

Kane surprising me with the loft.

Damn it, he will not soften me up over this mob thing. Nope. Not happening. Because what good is a loft if we're dead? And I'm not dying yet. There are too many people to kill to leave this soon. I suppose I can settle for putting them in jail. I do put people in jail. I just keep getting pitted against killers who try and kill me and leave me no options.

I enter our room to find some guy I don't know messing around the bed, checking under the mattress for who knows what he thinks Ghost might have done in here. It's ridiculous. "Get out," I order, and open the door to the loft and start the walk upward.

Kane's voice sounds behind me, a muffled exchange in Spanish I ignore but understand, though I'm amused by the fact that few people know that fact. I'm married to Kane, and I'm an FBI agent. Do they think I'm stupid? I actually hope they do. It's pretty much perfection to understand what those around you believe you do not. They say shit. I hold it against them.

I enter the upstairs, an exact replica of my prior loft, which translates to a desk with big white boards lining the walls. My phone buzzes for about the millionth time with a text message, and I sit down in one of the two chairs on the left-hand wall, or rather plop down. It's been a hellish day. I could place the desk between me and Kane, but why? I welcome confrontation.

I'm not hiding.

I snake my phone from my pocket and read through a dozen messages from Tic Tac, picking out what is important. Number one, the president is going to call me, so watch for an unknown number. Ellis is still offline. His phone pings at the Walker ranch with Elsa's phone and is not moving. What do I want Tic Tac to do about it? Lucas never contacted Tic Tac, and Tic Tac is freaking out. He's got an agency guy helping him track Elsa, but has given "her" limited information. So, the guy is a girl.

I'm about to call Tic Tac when Kane appears in the doorway, looking all Latin hotness and holding a bag of chocolate. It pisses me off. I set my phone on the table next to me and stand, angling toward him. "Chocolate will not save you."

He closes the short space between us and captures my hand, pressing the chocolate into my palm. "You love chocolate."

"Chocolate will not save you," I repeat, "or me. What the hell were you thinking, Kane?"

His chin lowers, and he releases my hand, stepping backward while I set the chocolate on the table next to my phone. The battle is on. And we're not leaving this loft until it's settled.

CHAPTER TWENTY

That step backward Kane just took doesn't infuriate me. It destroys me. That fight we had over him walking away to protect me isn't over, and I'm starting to think it's one I can't win.

"So this is how it is between us now, Kane?"

I see understanding flash over his face, and the next thing I know, his hands are firm on my shoulders as he rotates me and plants me against the wall, him in front of me, but he doesn't exactly cage me. Not if you don't count his fist planted on the wall on either side of my head, no part of him touching me.

"No to whatever you're thinking. *No*. But damn it, Lilah, at any point, any at all, are you going to ask me what I've done instead of deciding you already know?" he demands.

"You shut me out. It's not as if you've invited conversation. And at this point, you made a deal with the mob. That's all I need to know."

"Is it? Come on, bella. It's not always that simple, and you know it. You and I, we do what we have to do to survive in a world where most would not. That's what I did, and damn it, you are the one who lectured me about not letting my father get in my head. You told me to do what I do and take control. I took control. He just doesn't know it yet, but he damn sure will."

"And you think getting in bed with the mob was the way to do that?" I challenge. "We're battling the cartel, the Society, and now the damn mob."

"We're not battling any of them. We control them. Through the mob I own my father. Through my father I own the mob. And through you, we're on our way to the same with the Society."

"How does this control your father?"

"The mob has rebuilt. They're well-rooted in every place my father needs to be to make money. My uncle didn't have the balls to go to war with them. My father does. And the mob hates my father. He's why they had to rebuild."

"So you started a war? How do we not get in the middle?"

"I didn't start a war. I simply told the patriarch of the mob my father is back. They plan to end him before he comes for them."

"And if they can't?"

"I will."

I shake my head. "No. This changes nothing. *Again*, it leaves you in charge of the cartel."

"That's not true. If I kill my father, my role is cemented as his replacement. It's a claim to leadership, and I swear that bastard is setting me up for that. If the mob kills him and I play savior, staving off a war, it changes the dynamic. Instead of me being forced to take control or watch a battle of the worst human beings I know on this earth battle for control, the mob vows to respect an allegiance to my chosen successor."

"I really don't get why this gives you the right to walk away, but it doesn't matter. The cartel will accept you walking away. You're sure?"

"Positive."

"Because it's about money?"

"It's always about money."

"And you couldn't tell me any of this before you did it, why? No more secrets. Remember? No. No, apparently you don't remember at all. Maybe it's just not in your capacity to tell me before you do things. That's kind of your MO." I try to duck under his arm.

He blocks me, using his big body as a wall on either side of me and in front. "Are you really going there, Lilah? Back to that night? Because if you are, we have problems deeper than that grave I dug for your attacker. And it was pretty fucking deep."

"Don't turn this on me, Kane. I'll stand with you in the darkest recesses of Hell, but I want to walk into the fire with you, not get dragged. And I will. You have to know that."

"What do you think I was doing when I buried that body for you? Sending you to Hell by yourself?"

I breathe out emotions I wish were buried with that body. I don't know how we got back there now, and suddenly weird feelings and bad memories assail me. "I need space." I try to move again and shove at his chest. "Get off me."

"Not until you hear me out."

"You aren't saying anything. Not once have you made even a slight attempt to tell me why you shut me out."

"Your badge."

"You're my husband, Kane. They can't make me speak against you, so just stop already."

"I can't stop protecting you. I won't promise—"

"So now that's your excuse for keeping secrets? You're protecting me? Are we really there again?"

"Nothing about what I did today is a secret. I told you."

"After, and there was a reason for that. You had a plan A and a plan B."

"You know me like no other human being knows me. Why can't you just trust that I would do what is right for us, for you? *Fuck*, Lilah. I was going to tell you. Just not then. I needed—I can't let him near you, and that's exactly what happened. And yes, I would have done whatever it took to end this and protect you."

I can feel myself soften, guilt stabbing at me. "I didn't marry you because I wanted a protector. That's not who I am or what I want."

"I know you like I know my own smell, bella. You know that, right?"

"And your point?"

"Even you need to feel safe," he says, his hands framing my waist, warmth burning away the icy cold memories of the past. "I shouldn't have suggested leaving," he murmurs. "That's not who we are. That's not what we do."

"And yet—"

He cups my face and draws my mouth to his. "Don't do that. It's done. I'm sorry. *I'm sorry.*"

His breath is warm, and my anger has gone cold. "I tried really hard not to need you, you know that?"

"I know, bella. Believe me, I know." His mouth covers mine, and he still tastes of whiskey and worry, and sometimes, like now, Kane tastes of death. It's there tonight, the bittersweet promise that he will kill for me, and all I can do is answer with, *me too. I will kill for you.*

We're wild, ripping at each other's clothes, and at least once I almost fall down trying to get my pants off while he holds me up. Finally, he's buried inside me, my back to the wall and him in front of me, driving into me. The hard surface behind me grinds into my back, but I don't care if it cuts me and I start bleeding.

I just want more Kane.

At some point, though, I cry out from the pain, which is somehow oh so appropriate for us. Pain that is pleasure. That is me and this man all the way. Apparently, he doesn't think so, though, and we end up on the floor with me on top of him, a floor just as rough and punishing at his back while I'm just as rough and punishing on top of him.

Sometimes I think pain is what we do best to each other.

Just not today.

When we've reached that edge where the wall and floor, and his father and Ghost, don't matter, where there is only that ultimate moment of *us*, I collapse over the top of him, panting against his neck. I melt into him, relaxing in a way I can only relax with Kane—his fingers splayed between my shoulder blades. But we have all of thirty seconds before both of our phones start ringing at once.

And for the strangest moment, I'm standing on that beach so many years ago, after my attack, and there is blood in the water. There's death in the air, and when I push up and stare down at Kane, I see it in his eyes. He feels it, too.

CHAPTER TWENTY-ONE

"Mother of Jesus, can they not just wait a minute?" Kane mutters, rolling off of me and reaching for his pants while both our phones go silent.

But not for long.

We've accepted the inevitable, and I follow his lead and scramble for my clothing. There's no peace for the wicked, and we are most definitely the wicked. I'm not sure I'd have it any other way, though I'd take a little less cartel in our lives right about now. Ghost and Pocher are enough.

Once we're both dressed, I reach for my phone, prepared to navigate whatever waits on me, but apparently Kane isn't as ready. He catches my arm and gives me one of his intense, for me only looks, framed with the kind of hard edge he does so well. "You have to trust me." It's as much order as plea, a weird combination he manages to pull off a bit too often, considering it works for me.

"You're pretty much the only person I trust, Kane. I mean, yes, I trust Jay, but sometimes in the wrong way. I trust him to put himself in harm's way. Yes. Check. I trust him to—"

"*Lilah.*"

"I trust you, Kane."

"Are you sure about that?" he challenges.

"Why does this feel like a trick question?"

"Because as we've established, I know you, which means you're not going to hear what I'm about to say to you. You have the attention of not one, but two lethal killers."

"Three if you count Elsa, though I'm not sure I have her attention yet."

"*Lilah.*"

"*Kane.*"

"My father and Ghost aren't just killers. They're intelligent, calculating, successful killers, and that success stretches over time. They have staying power. And the biggest mistake you will ever make is to think they are like anyone you have ever faced."

"If I underestimated even one of the people I have faced, I'd be dead. And that whole Enrique tattling to daddy thing is not cool. If he chooses the wrong moment to defy me, that can get us killed."

"Cut him some slack, bella. Enrique knows the brutality of my father. He's seen it firsthand. I understand why he wanted to call me, and you should as well."

"He called you because he was afraid you'd kill him if he didn't."

"I might have, if I wasn't too dead to get the job done. My father loves a good distraction to a murder. Enrique knows that. He was as concerned for you as he was for me." There's a knock on the door, and his scowl could burn a hole in Hell.

With a Spanish curse, he releases me and heads for the door, rubbing the back of his neck in the process. I grab my phone, dismissing the topic of Enrique as I eye what appears to be *ten thousand* text messages from Tic Tac that started out normal and reasonable.

All three of the targets not attending my father's party are in DC. Maryland is less than an hour away. I'd expected Elsa to be in DC; only DC will be locked down after a director, one of their own, was murdered.

Maybe the party isn't in play after all.

I scan a few more messages. Chief Houston is asking about Murphy and the status of the case. DD, the ME on Murphy's case wants to know if I want to join in the autopsy. The ME in the Gomez case is asking the same thing. There's nothing from that little dweeb Lucas.

I'm back to more messages from Tic Tac, noting the rising level of agitation—*I need help, answer your phone, and for once answer your phone. Where is Lucas?* is another theme.

"The sketch artist will be here in thirty minutes," Kane informs me, stepping back into the room. "I told them to just have him wait, maybe give him that damn strawberry pie. I can't believe you got him pie, Lilah."

"That pie is so good, it distracted him. He forgot to try to kill me," I joke, and then on a serious note, "I don't know if he's really going after my father. I think it was a distraction." My cellphone rings in my hand, and I glance at the caller ID. "It's Tic Tac, and he's losing his shit on text message. I have to take it."

I plop down in the chair behind me and hit "answer," and before I can say a word, I'm blasted. "I thought you were handling Lucas?!" His voice squeaks with panic, and I've heard a lot of things from Tic Tac before, even panic, but never with the Mickey Mouse voice.

"What is going on with you, Tic Tac?"

"I don't know, Lilah," Tic Tac says, snark in his tone. "I've been shuffled all over the place, threatened, scared, and bodies are dropping like flies. Is Ellis dead, or dirty, and I'm now on his shit list?"

"Ellis isn't coming after you."

"You don't know that."

He's right. I don't know much. And we've been at this way too long, with too many lives on the line, for me to feel like I'm the stupid one right now. "You need to take a deep breath, Tic Tac. I am not going to let anything happen to you." Kane sits down in the chair next to me and makes a motion, encouraging me to add, "Neither is Kane." Which reminds me of just how far I went to protect Tic Tac. "I called freaking Rich for you, Tic Tac. Do you know what hell that brought on me?"

"I'm sorry if hell rained down on you for saving my life, Lilah."

I scowl. "What is going on with you? I think I need to meet this guy you're dating. You're just plain snarky these days."

"I'm not dating anyone, remember? We broke up because he couldn't take you calling me at all hours of the night. This job is going to kill me. I don't want to die."

"You're not going to die, and when this is over, I'll call your man and promise him to not call at all hours."

"You'd be lying."

"I'd mean it when I said it." My phone buzzes with a call, and I glance at the caller ID and show it to Kane, who smirks. He knows what's coming, and it's not gentle. "Enrique is calling, Tic Tac. He's with Pocher's security guy. I'll explain later, and you can continue being cranky when I do." I disconnect and then hit the speaker button to answer Enrique with, "Is he on the chopper?"

"Yeah, and I made sure he was scared shitless."

"Good," I say. "Now do it *again*."

"What?"

"Go back to Lucas' house and hold a fucking gun to his head until he does his job. He still hasn't called Tic Tac. He's supposed to be finding Elsa. Or Ghost. I don't give two fucks. Find one. Find the other. And feel free to play cartel gangbanger. Shoot him in the foot or cut his damn finger off."

"Does this mean I'm back on your good side?"

"No," I say, meeting Kane's stare. "It does not mean you're back on my good side. It just means I'm not going to kill you tonight. I might tomorrow." I disconnect and set my phone on the table between me and Kane. "He's not off my shit list."

"I'm aware," he assures me.

I sigh and press my lips together. "There's more going on that I don't understand."

"You mean with Ghost?"

"I mean with everyone and everything. Ghost is a part of this. Maybe more than we know. Maybe he *is* the distraction. Maybe that's what he's being paid to do."

"If that were the case, why would he kill Elsa's brother?"

"Because someone on the hit list wants Mark and Elsa dead, is what I'm thinking. Ghost is just using the number one assassin thing as a cover story."

"That computes to me. The question is, who's pulling the strings?"

95

I push to my feet and turn to face him. "The president called me, which is not a big thing. I asked him to call to ensure the VP is protected. It's the fact I told him Adams wasn't communicating, and I'd barely hung up with him, and Adams called me."

"That feels funny to you?" he asks. "Maybe it's simply that his boss just got mad and he responded to that anger and contacted you?"

"I don't know. Maybe Adams is just an arrogant power play dick, and nothing more, but Adams also told me Ellis called him and told him if he didn't contact him by a certain time to come for him. Why didn't Ellis say that to me? He was with me when he left."

"What are you thinking?"

"Whoever is in charge really wants me out of the way and in Maryland, which is why I'm not going to Maryland."

CHAPTER TWENTY-TWO

The sketch artist is about twelve—okay, maybe twenty—and sitting at our kitchen island eating pie, with milk in his glass.

"Have you lost your mind?" I murmur softly to Kane, both of us still standing in the archway.

"Why don't you find out?" Amusement lights his otherwise dark eyes, telling me he's oh so proud of himself right now. My husband is ridiculously arrogant. I should hate that about him, but I really don't. Sometimes it even makes me hot, but I'll keep that to myself.

As for the kid, we will see.

A few minutes later, I'm eating Cheetos, with orange fingers that prove they were a bad choice for a Purgatory snack, and answering the questions "Joey" asks me about Ghost.

Joey is Joey Ramirez, and he's well-spoken, bilingual, and wearing head-to-foot Gucci that screams of money. I'd ask him his story, but he's too darn focused on his work, and his work helps my work, which is going pretty shitty right now. Like if I were the actual trashman, shit would be in the can. Shit is most definitely in the can.

I wipe off my hands and then offer Kane some Cheetos to go along with the ridiculously expensive whiskey he's been sipping. I assume he's silently celebrating besting his father, though I think it's premature to assume success. We're not on a winning streak right now, and it sucks.

Kane lifts a hand to decline, the look on his face pure disapproval. Crazy man. Cheetos and whiskey sound pretty good to me, and a great way to make it through this process. I grab his glass and sip, the bite of smoke that follows burning me all the way down.

I choke with the punishment, and Kane laughs, low and taunting. "That's what you get for not asking first."

There's a definitive sexual innuendo to his words that has little ol' Joey glancing up, and then he clears his throat. "How's this?"

He flips his drawing around, and I'm stunned by the likeness to Ghost—chiseled cheeks, a full mouth, close-set eyes, and a sharp nose. "That's incredible," I say, pulling it closer. "I can't get over this. How did you learn to do this?"

"My mom was a profiler in Texas. The FBI recruited me out of college, but the pay was shit. I decided to start contracting out my services, and now I get *paid*."

"Out of college? How old *are you*?"

"Twenty-nine."

"You look—"

"Yeah, it's not the best with the ladies, but once I draw them," he wiggles his eyebrows, "they're all mine." He taps the drawing. "Any changes?"

I glance over at Kane, only to find he isn't here anymore. Frowning, I push off the barstool and motion to the drawing. "There's a slight dimple in his right cheek. I'll be right back." I grab the whiskey glass Kane has left behind and head into the living room. He's not there, but the patio door is open, and bitter cold air lifts the curtains and washes over me, sending a shiver down my spine.

I hurry to the door to find him standing far in the distance, near the ocean, where it has to be brutally icy, and he's not even wearing a coat. *Crazy man*, I think, baffled by the way he's disappeared on me. I set the whiskey glass down on the coffee table, hurry to the front door, and slide into my coat before snagging his and the glass.

It's a decent, biting trek to reach him, and once I'm there, I step in front of him, my back to the water, the crash of waves that follows moments later a reminder of the force of nature we cannot control. Too often, I've thought of Kane just that way—a force of nature I cannot control. I'm not sure I ever really want to anymore. Some part of me hungers for that part of him, even needs it.

I stare up at him, the splay of moonlight caressing his handsome features, sharply etched in some dark emotion I do not understand. If he feels the cold, it doesn't show. His hands are at his sides, fingers curled in his fists. I drop his coat and offer him the whiskey. He reaches for the glass, his hands folding over mine, and for a moment he just stares down at me, but he doesn't seem to be searching for anything. I think he's in his own head, processing whatever is going on, the information I'm not privy to, at least not quite yet. But for reasons I cannot explain, I dread what is to follow.

He accepts the glass and downs the amber liquid before stepping around me and hiking the glass as far as he can throw it. I turn to watch it hit the edge of the water, and for long minutes we just stand there, questions rattling at my brain. I'm really confused right now.

"You've seen this version of Ghost before," I assume.

"Yes."

"Why does that freak you out? You said he changes up his appearance. He just showed us the same version of himself. That feels expected?"

"I told you, he always conceals his features in some way, be it a mask, facial hair and sunglasses, a change of hair color. He keeps a distance, sets meetings at night, and does so in strategic locations. I was never sure who the real him was. None of those versions of Ghost match the sketch Joey drew."

"Okay I think I follow. You've seen the version of Ghost Joey created where?

"In public. I've randomly spotted him and the fact that it was several times sits strange to me which I'm certain was the intent. Ghost knew you'd have him sketched again. He knew I'd know I'd seen him in the past and I also know that means he's been too close for comfort. It was a warning, and an arrogant one at that. He's telling me he doesn't care if I see his face. He's untouchable, and I am not. You *are not*."

"It was a message from the Society."

"Yes. They're telling us that we might think we have the upper hand, but we do not."

"You mean Pocher is telling us."

"No. Pocher is nothing more than a figurehead. He wouldn't come at us unless the head of that snake told him to do it."

The degree of over I am with the Society cannot even be measured. I'm done, and the determination to make them done burns inside me, fire that doesn't need flame but rather a target. I try to step away from Kane, and he captures my arm. "Where are you going?"

"Somewhere I can kill at least one person. More would be preferable."

"You can't kill what you cannot see, who you do not know."

"I might not know this person, but Pocher does. And so, I bet, does my father. I'm confident I can find a way to make them talk, and it's way past time I stop holding back with them."

CHAPTER TWENTY-THREE

I attempt to step around Kane again, and he captures my shoulders. "Wait. Strategic moves only."

"Sometimes the most strategic moves involve shock and violence."

"I don't disagree, but you don't run into a snake pit and expect to survive, either. You trick the snakes, trap the snakes, and own the snakes. You know this."

"We're the ones getting owned. I'm done with this bullshit. *Done.*"

"At least talk through this with me. There are implications to the Ghost situation. You need to hear me out."

"I'm freezing my ass off, so if you want to try to slow me down and calm me down, do it inside. Or do arrogant CEOs who are now mob bosses not get cold?"

"I am not a mob boss, Lilah."

"If you control them, you own them, right?" I snatch up his coat and shove it at him, the act surprising him into losing his grip just enough for me to extract myself from his hold and step around him, with the house as my destination.

Kane catches up to me almost immediately, pulling on his jacket—apparently, he is human after all—but making no attempt to stop my path forward. With the damp, biting wind tormenting our bodies and the heat of the moment passing, it's just plain torture. My *husband* manages to reach the door before me, pulling it open and allowing me entry into the warmth of our home. The home I now share with him, and probably would have sooner, if not for the society. Maybe, just maybe, my mother would have been spending holidays with us as well.

I walk into the kitchen to find Joey in deep concentration as he works on a sketch. "I think we're done for the night, Joey," Kane says, stepping to my side.

Joey jolts slightly as if lost in his own world and straightens, putting eyes on us, realization washing over him. "All right, then." He pulls the page from his book and sets it face down on the table, pushing to his feet and giving Kane a tiny nod. "I'm available if you need me."

"I'll see you out," Kane offers and walks his direction. I step to the liquor cabinet in a nook beside the kitchen and select a whiskey I know isn't smoky. Once I've filled my glass, I sip, savoring the warmth as it slides down my throat while replaying Kane's take on the Ghost situation. Now that I'm warming up—and cooling off, so to speak—something about it doesn't sit as right as it did out there standing on the beach.

I walk to the kitchen island and set my glass down, slipping out of my jacket before I flip over the drawing Joey has created to find a new image. Holy wildness. This kid is talented. I told him about sitting across from Ghost, and he has drawn a profile image of me sitting on the couch, staring across the coffee table at Ghost. And as I stare at the image he's created, memories flood me.

While I was with Ghost, logically I believed one of us would kill the other. I would kill him. I believed he came to kill me. Why else would he show his face? But I never felt threatened, just the crackle of energy between us that came from being in the room with someone we each deemed a threat.

It was almost like respect.

And yet...I don't know what is wrong with me. I haven't even profiled Ghost, let alone had even a fleeting thought about the assassin who resembles that of a profiler. Maybe Kane isn't the only one rattled by his father showing up from his grave. I'm not thinking like me. I'm out of my own head and out of my zone. I squeeze my eyes shut and will my mind to go black, shutting out the noise and allowing nothing and no one but Ghost into my head.

When my eyes open, I let my assessment of Ghost flow.

He's a loner by necessity. He can't talk to anyone about his career. I think...years of his lifestyle have taken a toll. He needs human contact with someone he can be real with. Does he think that's me?

He *does*.

And he wants to honor that connection, no matter how fabricated it is, by giving me a gift. Perhaps that started as simply giving me his trust, and my story triggered a new plan that includes killing my father. Ghost never intended to kill me, which is why he had the lights set up on a trigger. He needed an escape. I think he really plans to kill my father.

My mind is racing, and I grab the sketch of Ghost, staring at his well-drawn eyes, the artistic mastery capturing the green, the haunted man beneath his own skin. I see him clearer now, a man who needs to be number one, who finds satisfaction in that ranking and the payday that comes with it. He wouldn't take a job that equates to taunting us. That's beneath him.

He really does want Elsa dead.

Kane walks back into the room, and the minute I lay eyes on him, I say, "Ghost is not working for the Society. I see why you think he is, though, I do, and the targets attending my father's party certainly lend to the idea that there's a Society presence, but I don't think there is one, not a direct link."

"Then why," he says, joining me at the island to my left and leaning an elbow on it as he angles toward me, "is Ghost playing games with you, Lilah? And don't tell me he's not. He is."

"I know it feels logical that he's doing it for a payday, but he's a killer, not a playdate."

"Then why, Lilah?"

"He thinks I'm like him, and I am not. He kills for money. I kill for survival and justice."

"He is obsessed with you, that's for damn sure, but stalkers often kill those they stalk."

"Those they stalk don't like to play with knives like I do, now do they?"

"Lilah—" I shift his direction and push to my toes to kiss him. "He won't hurt me, not yet, I promise. Focus on your father. I have a couple of killers to catch, and I officially have a plan to do it. I need to make a call."

I start to pull away, and he drags me closer and ravishes me with a kiss that leaves me breathless. "Too many people want us both dead, bella. You will stay close to me until at least some of them are dead."

"It'll be torture since you're such an arrogant, bossy asshole when you're worried, but," I pause for effect, "*okay.*"

"Okay?"

"Yes. Okay. Now I really have to make a call. I need to make sure Elsa answers the shoutout Ghost gave her by killing her brother." I push away from him and reach for my phone, punching in my brother's number.

"Lilah," Andrew greets on the first ring.

"Have you done the press conference?"

"It's in an hour at the courthouse."

"Good. I'll be there after all. I have something to say to Elsa that's really going to piss her off. So much so, she'll want to kill me."

Kane curses under his breath, and I can't help it.

I laugh.

CHAPTER TWENTY-FOUR

Kane is not amused by my laughter. "Oh come on, Kane. You're way too on edge over me being me. You need another drink."

"You're not wrong."

"Is it your father?"

"Ghost isn't helping the situation, but yes, it's my father. Until he's gone once and for all, I'll be on edge."

"You have a plan. It's a good plan."

"He'll have his own plan. On top of it all, I have a business meeting I can't miss in the morning."

"What kind of meeting?"

"The kind that keeps my oil business going, bella. No mob, cartel, or Society involvement. Which is where my focus should be in the first place, not on the rest of this bullshit. And you're right. I need a drink. You want one?"

"Me and booze on camera might be fun to watch, but I'll pass."

"You're not that bad," he teases and walks toward the bar. "Just almost that bad."

My cellphone rings where it's sitting on the kitchen island, an unknown caller flashing on my caller ID, which screams Ghost to me. *Fabulous.* Kane is never stressed, not in a visible way, and he is not going to be happy, but just as he has to do his job tomorrow, I have to do mine tonight. I answer the call, "Who is this?" I'm pleasant that way. I know Tic Tac would agree, especially in his current state of joy and happiness.

"The guy you spent hours terrorizing before putting me on a chopper," is the reply, in a deep male voice.

Pocher's head of security. Paul, I think. He's not memorable enough for me to remember his name, if I ever knew it. "Oh," I reply. *"You.* My people must have failed since you're calling me, and for the record, hours seems a bit exaggerated. Enrique wasn't with you that long, but apparently, he made the time count if it felt like hours." Kane reappears, two glasses filled with amber liquid sloshing about the sides in hand, and sets one in front of me.

He lifts his chin at the phone, a pinch of curiosity on his face that has me placing the call on speaker, and just in time for Kane to enjoy the show, it seems.

"Your cousin yelled at me in random outbursts," Paul, or whatever his name is, complained. "Worse, he flashed a gun around that he didn't know how to use when he did. He could have killed us both."

"He's quite irritating, and I agree that at times his very presence can terrorize a person. I mean, I for one can only take so much stupidity."

Kane sits down and sips his whiskey, amusement lighting his eyes, his stress banked, at least for now. I'm entertaining, if nothing else.

Paul grunts and says, "I want to talk about election night."

"What about it?"

"Max Oliver is one of our largest donors. His place in the Hamptons is sixty-four thousand square feet. He has private security that's top notch."

"Why do I care what Max Oliver has on his property?"

"I want to move the party there. We can have the three targets stay on property."

"Are you asking me, or telling me?"

"You're the FBI agent handling the killer. Isn't it your job to help me secure a safe event?"

"Well, considering you got kidnapped by Lucas, I think it's valid to believe you need help doing your job and protecting my father."

"Has anyone ever told you you're a bitch?"

Kane silently laughs. I shrug. "I am. Thank you. And despite that good news for you, I don't plan to allow the assassin to be an issue that long."

"It's only days away."

"Your point?"

He makes a frustrated sound and rather abruptly hangs up. I have that effect on some men. I've already dismissed him, refocusing on Kane. "I need to get Tic Tac here where he feels safe. The minute we lured him to the city, we left. I'll have him stay with Lucas."

"And that will make him feel safe?"

"If you have Enrique stay with them."

"You're really trying to get rid of Enrique, aren't you?"

I see no reason to pretend otherwise, which makes my answer a simple, "Yes," and then I move on, "which reminds me. Where are Kit and Jay?"

"I sent Jay to check into a hotel. He'll be back. Kit's staying out of our hair, but he's here, securing the property. He'll be waiting on us to take us to the press conference."

"Securing the property from Ghost," I say flatly.

"From whoever the fuck dares try to enter. Apparently, you're about to invite Elsa over to kill you."

"I need her to actually be able to get in if we're that lucky."

"That means Ghost can get in," he counters. "Hard no."

"We're already locked down like Fort Knox. Easing it right now would be better than aiming higher."

"When there's a threat, you change things up; you don't give them the chance to know what you do not want them to know. Ghost studies his targets."

"I've told you, I'm not a target for Ghost."

"I might be. He's obsessed with you. Maybe he wants me out of the way."

"No," I say immediately. "It's not that kind of obsession. It's—it's just not." I wave off the topic. "I need to call Tic Tac. Can you get a chopper set-up for him and have the men with him escort him?"

"Is Jack coming?"

"I cannot believe I'm even saying this." I down the contents of the whiskey glass. "Yes. We'll bring Jack. I cannot believe I'm even saying this."

"You just said that."

"It's worth repeating. He's smart, too smart for my own good at times, but Tic Tac leans on him, and we need an extra brain on this." I grab my coat. "I'll call Tic Tac on the way to the press conference. I really need to get there and talk to Andrew in advance. Knowing my dumbass brother, he hasn't even thought of the potential that Elsa might show up at the press conference with her sniper gun."

Kane responds to my concern by calling in discreet manpower and reinforcements, which is fine by me. Maybe they'll kill her so I don't have to, because this isn't going to be pretty.

CHAPTER TWENTY-FIVE

A few minutes later, I'm in the back of the SUV, and the instant I connect with Tic Tac, he's at me again. "Enrique is holding a gun on Lucas. You know that, right?"

"He deserves it. He kidnapped Pocher's head of security. Apparently, he wants to die, and it might be me who kills him, so you can't hold that against me. It's easy to see he deserves it. You do not. We're bringing you here with us. You'll be as safe as a baby kangaroo in her mommy's belly."

"To stay where?"

"With Lucas and Enrique and a team of Kane's people."

"You mean a team of cartel members?"

I bristle at that. Kane is not the cartel, and I don't have to look at Kane to feel his agitation. "Are you putting in a special request for cartel members? Should I tell Kane you want the nastiest cartel members possible to guard you?"

There's a moment of silence in which I can feel Tic Tac's panic before he bursts out with, "No. No. No. Stop it, Lilah. And don't go telling Kane I said something I didn't say."

"You said—"

"I didn't. *I didn't*. I'm fine with Lucas and Enrique. And now for a poorly timed request. Can Jack come? He's been here with me all this time, diving through the files."

"You need me, Lilah," Jack calls out. "I'm your secret weapon."

That makes me feel like I'm being stabbed in the eye over and over. "Tell him to shut up or I'll say no."

"Quiet, Jack," Tic Tac whispers, a plea in his voice that drives home how rare his earlier outburst was with me. "He'll behave. And he's helpful."

"How?"

"You know what, Lilah, *I need* for once. Can you not give me what *I need*?"

"*I need* to know where every one of the six people on my list, outside of the VP, is right now."

109

"I texted you that hours ago. The two that are not the VP and not going to the party were highlighted."

"Just tell me."

"Congressman Stevens is in her home state of California. Senator Soto is in her home state of Texas. Soto has a husband who's a retired Navy SEAL and two brothers in the Army. She's well-known for her love of guns."

"I like her already, but she's a hard target. Elsa won't go after her first. Stevens is another story."

"I can ask Rich to go look after her."

Rich is such a pain in my ass—a crazy stalker, worse than Ghost in some ways. Because he does want me. Because he would hurt Kane if he had the chance and end up dead trying. I skip the Rich question. "You made sure the targets are all aware of what's going on?"

"Yes. Of course I did, and so you know, Ellis had already called them. And no, his phone hasn't moved."

He called them, but he's MIA. Either he's dead or he set things up to look like he became Elsa's victim. "What about diner girl?"

"Nothing."

"Tell Jack if he wants to win me over, find her. Yes, this is a test."

"Does that mean Jack can come with me to the Hamptons?"

My phone buzzes with a call. "Yes," I confirm, the word choked from me. "I have to go. I'm holding a press conference on the Mark Walker murder. Kane's team will get you here, and as long as you're nice to them, they won't cut your fingers off or otherwise torture you."

I don't even look at Kane. He's amused. Of course he's amused. I glance at the caller ID, find Lucas on the line, and answer, "How badly are you hurt?"

"He's holding a flipping gun on me. I was already working, but Tic Tac is distracting."

"I told you to calm him down. You did not."

"You told me to do my job, and I did. Ellis has a connection to Elsa outside of what you already know."

Now he has my attention. "Which is what?"

"His daughter went to school with Elsa."

"You're fucking kidding me?"

Kane's gaze rockets to mine, and I tell him. "Elsa went to school with Ellis' daughter."

"That's not good."

He's right. It's not. I return my attention to Lucas. "What else?"

"Get the gun off of me and tell him to stop pinching my damn leg, and I'll work on finding Elsa and Ghost."

"Not even you can find Ghost. Elsa's coming into town. Find her when she gets here. And I need to know if Adams is dirty."

"Like I said—"

"Put Enrique on."

"Hold on."

"Lilah," Enrique greets.

"Back off, but remind him you're there, and often."

"Copy that."

I disconnect as Kit pulls into the courthouse, a white structure with tall pillars and I can already see the press everywhere. "There's a staff parking lot around back." I say, and once he nods his understanding, and I use every moment I have until I'm in front of the press. I punch in Adams' number, but I don't expect him to answer, as he never has in the past, and especially not with a flight from California to Maryland likely in progress. To my surprise he answers. "Well timed," he greets. "I just landed in Charlotte. I'm flying private from here. It's the only way I get there tonight."

"Any word from Ellis?"

"No. None. I have a team watching Elsa's place, but the only movement is what appears to be a maintenance crew. I made the call to have them hold back until I get there and assess the situation. I don't work with those guys daily. I won't risk Ellis' blind devotion."

You hold on action, and if Ellis is captive, time is not on his side, and he could die. You go in prematurely, he dies.

Or he helps kill your team. It's a hard call, but holding back is probably a smart one. Refocusing on the point of this call, I ask, "Do you know?"

"Know what?"

"Well, for starters, *anything*? Did Ellis tell you about Clyde, Elsa, Mark, and the hit list?"

"Yes."

"Mark's dead. Long story I don't have time to tell. I'm at the courthouse for a press conference related to Mark's death. I'm betting that Elsa is about to lose her shit when she finds out and comes here."

"Who killed Mark?"

I explain the whole Ghost thing before I circle back to him. "Do you know about the link between Ellis and Elsa? Did he tell you?"

"He did not. What fucking link? What am I walking into?"

My gut tells me I have to tell him. It's necessary knowledge that helps him stay alive. If he's dirty, he'll pay. I'll make sure of it. "Elsa went to school with the director's daughter."

"Holy hell," he breathes out. "You think Ellis is dirty and working with her?"

"Or playing bleeding heart, trying to save her, which might well have gotten him killed. If Ellis is with Elsa, I'm not sure how she will react to Mark's death. She lost her mother tragically a few years back. Then her father. Now her brother."

"In other words, she's armed and emotional. The worst kind of opponent."

"Exactly. And for the record, I have questions about why Ellis would trust you when he supposedly does not know you well. Expect me to ask them if you live." A knock sounds on my window, which will of course be my brother, since he has the timing of a two-year-old at all times. "I have to go."

"I have a good answer," he says.

"Doubtful, but I'll hear it before I kill you."

112

"You know your job is to arrest people. We're going to work on that, Special Agent Love-Mendez."

He hangs up on me.

And I can't help but wonder if him using Love-Mendez is meant to suggest my name, and my marriage is why I leave a trail of bodies behind me. If so, he has no idea how wrong he is with that premise. The bloodbath that is my life is all me.

CHAPTER TWENTY-SIX

The knocking on my window has grown more incessant, and I roll it down to find my brother standing there. Imagine that. Andrew being a nag even without words. "Have you ensured you're ready if Elsa shows up?" I ask, as if I were the one knocking on his window.

Irritation tics in his jaw. "Do I look like a fucking idiot?"

"Do you want me to answer that?"

"I love you too, you little bitch, which is why I wasn't risking you getting killed. I need you around to torment me. Get out of the damn SUV. We need to just get this over with." He opens the door, and I eye Kane over my shoulder, a question in the action.

"I'll catch up, bella. Be *careful*."

Translation: He needs an update on his team, and Ghost is likely present and closer than I expect. I give a short nod and exit, shutting the door behind me. "Kane has some of his men on the perimeter," I explain softly. "And before you get prickly, I'm not saying you're not doing your job, but one sniper can level the crowd."

"I've replayed that exact scenario you just mentioned in my head a hundred times. I had the microphone placed in a location where we'll be sheltered. I wanted to put up bulletproof glass, but I knew you'd lose your shit."

"You mean the audience would lose their shit."

"That too. Change of topic. My replacement is here. I warned him you're going to bust his balls."

"Isn't it great how well we know each other? Where is he so I can make you right?"

"He's waiting on us at the podium. I'd ask what I need to know, but I guess he needs to know, too." He scrubs his jaw. "I can't believe I'm leaving."

"I can't believe you're working for Dad."

"You know why I'm doing this, Lilah."

"The chief in our little town has been a Love job for a long time. Only one of you is good at your job and has a moral compass. But you're about to be sucked into a hell pit with Dad and Pocher. They'll try to corrupt you, and power is addictive."

"The idea of you stabbing me and Kane burying me is a pretty big deterrent, let me tell you."

"First, if you'd become that shitty of a person, I'd have someone else do it. You are still my brother. Also, you're still sleeping with that bitch. Proof you are indeed corruptible."

"Stop already. I'm not marrying her, I was never even thinking about it, and I haven't seen her in weeks, and right now, I'm feeling weird about handing over my job. Let me just live in that feeling, will you?"

"That feeling sucks. And you—"

"Don't say I did this to myself. That sucks, too."

I grunt. "I'm biting my tongue right now, just so you know. What's your take on the new guy so far?"

"I told you, I like Dave Taylor. He's a temporary placement right now, though, so we'll have time to test what seems to be an honorable record."

"Have you ever heard about putting an avocado in a paper bag to ripen it?"

"Why are we talking about avocados?" He holds up a hand. "Don't answer. I got it. Because it's you. Yeah. I have. It works damn well, but you have to be careful, or it gets too soft too fast."

"And rotten to the core. It happens fast. Don't ever forget that, big brother, especially when you're headed into the garden of rotten, which is all things Dad and Pocher. Take me to your avocado."

He laughs. "Should we call him Mr. Avocado?"

"Better than Mr. Potato Head. And you do need to know a few things I'd rather you hand out with discretion. You, not me. This Taylor dude needs to earn trust." I update Andrew on Ellis, Adams, and election night.

"I heard about election night," he says.

"What do you think?"

"I think it's going to make my little town into a zoo, but it won't be the first time. We know how to manage it. What do *you* think?"

"Feels like our turf. I think I like it."

"Any updates on Ghost?" he asks.

"We want what he wants. Elsa. We're going to help him get her in a big way. And quite possibly piss her off in the process."

"So you said. Should I prepare the new guy?"

"Nope. Let's see how he rolls."

"Should we check on Kane?"

"Kane doesn't need a babysitter, but the new guy might. Let's get this over with. The sooner we get the word out, the sooner we get our bait set, and I'm too tired to stab a bitch tonight. I will, but I'd enjoy it more later. I need sleep."

"Yes to all of the above. Sleep won't make you have a winning personality, but it makes you less of a bitch, so I'm all for it." He motions me forward, and as we walk, we pass several of his deputies who wave at me. They like me or they fear me. Either way works for me.

We're almost to the edge of the building, about to step into the heat of the press's attention, when a tall, good-looking man with wavy brown hair steps in front of us. He's in uniform, but not the local gear, and when his blue eyes land on mine, I know he's not only the new chief; he's not my friend.

"You're the new acting chief in town," I say, making sure that "acting" is emphasized.

"I could have sworn that was you," he retorts dryly, with a distinct southern accent, "since you're always taking over. I'm not your brother. That shit won't fly with me."

"You're out of line," Andrew snaps.

"You're also not in charge if I claim jurisdiction," I say, "which I'm about to do for all the world to see."

"Who and what gives you that right?"

"My purdy badge," I say all sugar sweet, in my best southern accent, which is pretty good if I might say so myself. "You ever heard the one about the southern boy who rushed into a bar all pissed off? 'Who painted my horse's balls red?' he declared." I act it out. I'm enjoying this. "A big ol' biker dude, who might as well have been a basketball player, he was so tall, declared, '*I did*. What about it?' The cowboy knew he was beat, and he cut his eyes to his boots as he said, '*He's ready for the second coat*.' My purdy badge is the big ol' biker dude. And you're the cowboy."

"Typical FBI agent, always trying to intimidate someone."

"Oh, I am not your typical FBI agent. I'm much worse. Now, how about that press conference?"

CHAPTER TWENTY-SEVEN

As I step up to the podium, cameras flash and film rolls. Time for the show, but not a script. I just wing it, dig in deep, and wade through the same bullshit I'm about to spew. "Good evening, everyone," I start. "Many of you know me before I ever introduce myself. I am FBI Agent Lilah Love-Mendez. I grew up here. I went to school here. And yes, my mother graced many small and big screens, right here in our small community and beyond. My father, of course, is the future governor of our great state." There are cheers from the fools who believe him a good man with aspirations to help them and their state prosper. I'd call them fools, but my father wears the disguise of an angel while playing with the devil. I go on. "My brother is your beloved chief." More cheers. So many cheers, and as a sister, I am filled with pride. I leave out the part where he's leaving, but there are shouts of, "Don't go! We need you!" *There you go, Taylor, and fuck you, too.*

"And most importantly," I continue with a dramatic pause, "I am a citizen of this town, where my memories run deep, my devotion deeper, and my addiction to Micki's Diner's strawberry pie has brought me great joy." There are a number of agreements from the audience before I add, "I begin this press conference with my history simply so you know my commitment to this town, to our people, our community. And so, let's get to it.

"Mark Walker has been found dead in his home. There is no threat to you or your loved ones. This was a calculated attack, and the victim was known to the attacker. We are clear on the motivation, which I will not talk about today, as we're dealing with an ongoing investigation. But our knowledge of motivation for the crime allows us to offer assurance that you should not be afraid. To be clear, I am officially declaring jurisdiction over this case. And the answer to why? There's a political component that crosses state lines. I will not be talking about that component in any further detail, either.

"I want to assure you that we are hunting this killer. I want to assure Elsa, Mark's sister, that we, that *I*, will find this brutal monster. Elsa is not present, nor is she communicating, but I know she must be hurting. She's a member of the military, trained to honor and serve, to protect, and she didn't protect her own brother. That has to cut. I can assure you she blames herself, but I do not. I am sure you do not, either. She's not a suspect, and when self-blame is involved, it's often hard to face the public. But she'll grow stronger again, and when she does, she'll come and say her goodbyes."

I look directly into the camera in front of me. "If you're out there, Elsa, don't worry. I'll do the job for you. I will take care of this. I will pass judgment, and I will do what you cannot. *That's all,* everyone. No questions."

With that, I walk away from the podium and exit the stage to have Kane and Andrew frame me as we walk toward the car. Kit and Raz are at our rear. Jay waits for us in the not-so-far distance at the SUV. "Should Raz be around us, Kane?" I whisper softly.

"Yes," he replies, letting me know that's all he's saying in the present company, but he has a plan.

"You just invited an assassin to come kill you, Lilah," Andrew laments, leaning forward to look at Kane. "Did you know about this?"

"Better to get a warning than be surprised," Kane comments dryly. "She just warned us about what is coming."

"Better she come after me than someone else," I comment.

"I feel like I've heard that too many times, Lilah," my brother snaps.

"You have," Kane states. "On that we agree, Andrew."

We've just reached the SUV, and Kane and Andrew have huddled up with me to talk when I'm saved the safety lectures by the new, soon-to-be-gone, I predict, Chief Taylor."

Kit and Raz step in front of him, and I lean in toward Kane. "Andrew's replacement," and then call out, "He's good, guys. He's the new chief."

They part and open a gap for Taylor, who strides the remainder of his walk toward us. "Chief," I say, "meet Kane Mendez, my husband."

Kane tilts his chin in greeting, and Taylor stares at him with the kind of hatred that comes with a history I should know about but don't. One glance at Kane, and I sense he has no clue what is going on, either. Could it be that the cartel did Taylor wrong in some personal way, and he believes that means Kane?

Another beat passes, the heaviness of Taylor's anger hanging in the air. Taylor might not be my friend, but he's Kane's enemy.

My enemy, through Kane.

"Problem, Chief?" I ask, my tongue whiplash sharp.

He jolts himself, a physical shake, and then looks at me, the haze of anger still lingering in his eyes. "What just happened? Why did you just set yourself up as bait?"

"I'll fill you in," Andrew states, glancing at me with a question in his eyes and handing me back the power he seems to want me to have right now. He doesn't like what just went down any more than I do. "If," he adds, "my sister approves of me releasing the information?"

"Just the basics," I say, limiting Taylor's influx of knowledge, before I turn away from them to enter the vehicle. Kane immediately follows me, and soon Kit is across from us and Raz is up front with Jay.

"What the hell was that?" I ask, rotating to face Kane.

"I have no idea," Kane replies, confirming what I already suspected. He was clueless. "I assume it's cartel related. It's not an unfamiliar reaction with those who believe my father and I are the same person." He's already snaked his phone from his pocket. "I'm going to have my tech guy search for a history."

"Macom?"

"Yes, Macom."

Macom is a German hacker who actually lives in Germany and seems to be about as good as Lucas. He's expensive, though, and Kane doesn't like working with someone outside his easy reach.

"I was worried about Raz being seen with us," I murmur softly, returning us to the question I'd asked before we got into the vehicle. "If he does what you plan for him to do, you connect yourself to him."

"In the cartel is my power to control the Society. And when I make it clear I'm tight with the patriarch of the mob, that increases two-fold."

"It's going to cause Taylor to come at you hard and fast."

He reaches up and slides my hair behind my ear. "Good thing I have an FBI agent to protect me." His lips curve, but his phone buzzes with a text message, and he glances down and laughs. "It's your father." His gaze lifts to mine. "He wants to know if I can help him with a security threat on election night. He doesn't trust Pocher's plan. And, of course, my answer will be yes."

His cellphone rings, and he grimaces. "Macom. It's never good when he calls that fast." He answers the call, listens a minute, murmurs a few words, and hangs up.

"It's not good," he says. "When Taylor was in Texas, El Paso to be specific, his wife and baby got in cartel crossfire. They were killed."

Pretty much the entire vehicle curses, and I feel a twist in my chest. Taylor was a dick to me, but he sees me as an extension of Kane, and Kane the kingpin of the monsters who killed his family.

"Taylor was transferred to Long Island to get him away from the incident, as he was struggling with volatile behavior," Kane adds. "Which is not so unexpected, considering all, but something like that changes a man. He's trouble. We'd be good to prepare for him to bring that trouble to us, but it's not the first time we've dealt with someone like him. It won't be the last."

I don't hate Taylor just yet, not with this fresh knowledge to guide my direction with him, but he's dangerous. None of us can forget that.

Ever.

CHAPTER TWENTY-EIGHT

We finally have some time alone, just me and Kane, and I don't even feel the need to be in Purgatory. This case ends with Elsa and Ghost, in different ways, and if I find Elsa, I find Ghost again.

After having our favorite pizza joint deliver, we retreat to our bedroom and sit at a small corner table we often use to eat, enjoying the quiet, the calm before the storm. We aren't completely alone; we never are. Kit's here, but that's the norm, and he has his own room on the lower level. He also knows how to play invisible to us and our enemies.

Jay and Raz are on their way to pick up Tic Tac and Jack from the airport. After which, Raz and Enrique will stay the night at Lucas' place and allow Enrique a break. Okay, they're protecting Lucas too, I suppose, but he seems to be the one inviting the trouble, so fuck him right now.

I take a bite of a slice of pineapple, bacon, and jalapeño pizza while Kane fills our wine glasses with a red blend that's a favorite of ours. "What the hell was Lucas thinking?" Kane asks, setting the bottle down.

"He's gone off the deep end over the idea of Murphy being in that airport photo right before the crash. He's not in his right mind, Kane. He needs some grace."

"You saw the photo, too, and you haven't gone off the deep end."

"I did that way back on a beach with a blade in my hand."

"He's not you, Lilah, and his drinking problem is proof of that, if you need more than the general way he handles life. And you. I won't apologize for being possessive of my wife around a man who makes it obvious he wants to fuck her. And him pretending to be family to get close to you is the sign of a low individual."

"I don't think it's like that at all. I believe he attaches himself to me because he has no one else. He lost his parents."

"You lost your mother, and your father isn't a father at all."

"But I always had you, Kane, at least for as long as I can remember."

"You had me, even before you were willing to admit you needed me. But you're making excuses for him, and you do him no good by doing so. He has a track record of irrational decisions."

He's not wrong. The high target hacking, excessive drinking, kidnapping people.

"I'm not even sure it's safe to allow him all the knowledge you do, bella. At some point, when he's drunk, will he sell off the information?"

"He has money."

"So did a lot of people until drugs and drinking made them do stupid shit and lose it, often a lot of it."

"I already told him he has to go back to rehab. And enough on Lucas. *Please.*"

His expression tightens, and he reaches for his glass. "For now. I'm out of patience with him, Lilah."

I push onward. "How long is Raz staying around?"

"Until your father and Pocher have met him and know he's submissive to me. That way, when he becomes the head of the cartel, they still see that as me. Ultimately, until my father is dead."

"When will that be?"

"That's on the mob. It could be a day, or a week, or maybe longer, but I urged expediency, considering how much damage my father can do in a short time."

"You really think your father will act against you in that time?"

"He wants my attention. That's why he cornered you. If I don't give it to him, he'll escalate his efforts."

"What does he expect from you after visiting me?"

"He wants me angry and in his face, demanding he honor the hands-off of our women rule when he follows no rules. But that's a weak response he'll obliterate me for."

"What's the strong response?"

"Killing him, which is what I've arranged. Outside of that, I need to do nothing. It sends a message that his interruption meant so little to us, we barely remember it. He is not a threat. He is not king."

"Won't that poke the bear?"

"Yes."

"Yes? Just yes? Won't he escalate if we don't react?"

"I've been thinking about that. I think we should play up how he wanted to get to know you, rather than the threat in his actions. I, we, could invite him to your father's party," he suggests.

I blink. "What? Are you serious?"

"He claims he and Pocher are tight, implying he's talked to him, which I do not believe, but he showed himself in public. That means he intends to stay, and he's feeling cocky as he's aligned with someone powerful."

"Like Pocher."

"Exactly. We have to find out if that's a real relationship. We look stupid and disposable, a gnat to be swatted, if we don't know what is happening."

"I can't believe my father or Pocher would want a kingpin back from the dead at my father's party."

"They won't, which sends a subtle message to my father. It will put him in his place in the shadows. We don't even have to actually invite him. I can tell him we'll see if we can clear his invitation with Pocher and your father. He'll object. No matter what, he'll know he's not welcome, but we'll make it clear we know, too."

"Do we tell Pocher and my father you're inviting him?"

"No. I can read my father. I'll know if he's talked to Pocher. When he declines, we'll invite him to dinner."

"Will he come?"

"He'll come, if he's alive to come."

I down the contents of my wine glass, meant to be sipped, the rush of wine and the voice of my father in my head rushing over me. *Let them believe they're in control. The fact that they don't know the truth is a weakness.* Kane's effectively using my father's strategy against our enemies, but will my father see through it for that very reason?

Or is he perhaps using that very strategy against *us*, and we're the ones being played? It's a horrible thought, and I grab a new slice and stuff my face with it, looking for comfort when I'm more likely to find a bellyache.

And another murder.

The room might smell of pizza, but murder is in the air.

CHAPTER TWENTY-NINE

Killers know killers.

Those words replay in my mind long after Kane falls asleep. I lay awake with Ghost on my mind, aware that his obsession with me is not normal, but neither am I, and that's the point.

Ghost knows I'm not normal.

Ghost knows I'm a killer.

And while, for the most part, I've found a way to accept that part of me that can kill, justifying it as being part of my job, this is mostly to the credit of Kane, who still manages to see the balance of light in me to his dark. I often cannot any longer. But having Ghost see the dark, really see it, seems like something that should bother me.

But it doesn't, and I tell myself that's simply survival. I need Ghost to know what I'm capable of doing, who I can be, and how much control I have to be able to turn it off and on at will.

Mostly.

But I can't arrest someone like Ghost. He knows too much about Kane. He knows too much about me.

That leaves only life or death for Ghost.

I'm not sure either is a good answer.

CHAPTER THIRTY

There is blood in the water...

I blink awake with a gasp, having dreamt of the night I killed my attacker, the fog of the drugs having done nothing to douse the fury and helplessness of my attack. Kane had been right to bury the body. I wouldn't have gone to jail, but I would have been considered mentally compromised. Even if I'd been reinstated after counseling, every step I took would have been analyzed.

Kane rolls over and wraps himself around me, his scent flaring in my nostrils, and for a moment, I sink against him and allow myself the vulnerability of needing this, of being *human*. Once again, he's brought me back to him. And this moment has Elsa sliding into my thoughts, and I realize I've been distracted by Ghost. I don't even know if Elsa has a boyfriend, or girlfriend, or whatever. Does she have anyone helping her, supporting her?

I roll away from Kane and grab my phone from the nightstand, punching in the autodial for Tic Tac. "Lilah," he murmurs groggily. "You know it's five a.m.?"

"No, but thanks for the time update. Do you do temperature, too?" I don't wait for his grumble. "I need—"

"Stuff. Right. What?"

"Elsa. Does she have a boyfriend? Girlfriend? Close friend? Someone that might help us look for her? Or someone we need to be ready for because she has help?"

"I know the answer. And that answer is no. She dated a guy in the military who got killed in a chopper accident."

"Fuck. She's nothing but tragedy."

"Agreed. She seems to have stayed to herself after she lost him."

"Where did he live?"

"Maryland."

"That checks out," I say, and I sit up to find Kane scooting up the headboard, not at all surprised about my abrupt burst into action. He leans over and kisses me, to whisper, "Coffee."

I cover the receiver and say, "Please."

Lucas comes on the line. "Morning, cousin, and fuck you for getting us up this early."

"At least you're sober enough to be up, and after what you pulled yesterday, I hope you're hungover as hell."

"Fuck you."

"You already said that."

"You deserve to hear it again," he grumbles. "What are we doing right now?"

"This is how Lilah works," Tic Tac explains. "Her mind starts working and she calls me. And I guess you, too."

"Why the hit list now, not back when Clyde killed himself?"

"Things simmer and burn," Lucas replies. "And when it burns, it burns really fucking badly."

He's not talking about Elsa right now, but himself. "There's usually a trigger. Try to find out what it is. Maybe she found out Clyde was murdered."

"That would make sense," Tic Tac says. "We'll get on it."

"I need to know if Elsa had ties to the Hamptons."

"She did," Tic Tac replies. "When she and her brother were kids, they came up here for Christmas. It was a tradition. And I only know that because Jack was on Elsa's socials for the firing range. She posted a photo of her and her family, way back when she and Mark were kids, with a note about the tradition."

Good ol' Jack, I think. He's irritating *as fuck*, but efficient. At the moment, his savvy feels worth the torture, but then again, I'm not enduring said torture right now. "Find out where they stayed when they were here or favorite spots. Maybe places Mark frequented. Elsa's not going to go to Mark's house, not unless she's stupid, and she's not. She'll go someplace that feels safe. *If* it's Elsa. We still don't really know for sure. I'm going to shower. I sincerely hope you are too, Lucas, considering you were disgusting last night. Call me or text me." I disconnect.

Kane walks into the room, shirtless, in pajama bottoms, with two steaming cups in his hands. I throw my legs over the edge of the bed, and he sits down next to me. "Morning, bella."

"Morning," I say, sipping the warm brew. "Delicious. You made my favorite hazelnut coffee."

"Seemed like you needed it. What woke you up so abruptly?"

"My mind attacked me with randomness. You know, I assumed that the reason Elsa and Mark's phones are both in Maryland means they wanted an alibi for the murders."

"It would have worked if Mark hadn't ended up dead."

My brows dip, and I'm not sure why my mind is pushing back. "Yes. True."

"What are you thinking?"

"You told me I was assuming, and that's unlike me. Am I wrong to assume Elsa is the assassin? No," I say before he can answer. "Ghost is after Elsa. It's Elsa."

"Ghost is a self-serving narcissist. That frames everything he does. He's either the killer after a payday or a killer after a payday. That's all he knows. Either Elsa is on the hit list, or she is the hit list. There's no other reason Ghost would be here."

Me, I think.

He might have come for Mark, or Elsa, or both, but is he lingering for me? I'm not saying that to Kane. I don't say it, but it's on my mind. It's still on my mind after I've showered and Kane has headed off to his meeting.

Dressed in my serious FBI gray pantsuit with a black silk blouse underneath and high heels I could slice a throat with, I stand in Purgatory and just think. And think some more.

I'm missing something, and I'm going back to Mark's place to figure out what.

CHAPTER THIRTY-ONE

I'm trying to be good. I really am.

Kit and I order egg white omelets and avocado toast from a local favorite breakfast joint, sitting at the kitchen island to enjoy a healthy start. I mean truthfully if I'm going to die a bloody death sooner than later, I'm not sure why I care if it's with clogged arteries. However, I do want to be physically capable of making sure whoever kills me dies with me. And of late, I haven't been training or eating right, a detail Kane pointed out before he left for work. *A blade takes skill and strength to kill with, Lilah. You must be ready for anything that comes your way. What if I don't get here in time the next time you're attacked? And there will be a next time.*

He's right. It's been two weeks since I sparred with him, and just as long since I hit the weights. No sleep, shitty eating, and zero training, makes for a live girl finding herself dead. I do not like weakness, certainly not in myself. And I swore I'd never allow myself to be as easily held down as I was on that beach that night.

The only blood in the water will be the asshole's who tries to attack me. "We need to talk about Jay," I comment after a bite of my omelet.

"I thought it was Enrique you have a problem with."

I ignore him and stay focused. "He's too good for all of us."

"Enrique? What the fuck?"

"Do not act slow," I say pointing my fork at him, "you know I'm talking about Jay."

"When Enrique defied you and called Kane, Jay would not have. He would have been right there with you, risking the wrath of Kane. Kane would have been pissed but ultimately okay with it because that would mean you had someone that loyal to you. But for the record, Enrique has seen some shit with Kane's father that no human should ever experience. He was afraid for him and you."

"I know he's loyal and that's why I don't want him to end up dead."

"Careful," he says, "someone might think you have a heart."

"I also have a gun."

"And yet you always find a knife."

"That's me showing restraint. I need to get Jay trained and hardened up. I want whoever it is to try to scare him off or toughened up."

"I know a guy but he'd need Jay with him for a good month."

"Does Kane know him?"

"Yes."

"Will Jay survive him?"

"I think he's tougher than you think, Lilah. And the police academy does not prepare him for our world. It's wasting his time and yours."

"Make it happen then. And speaking of loyalty, why aren't you with Kane?"

"Raz is with him. And Raz doesn't fuck around. Kane's safe with him."

"Kane is determined to flash him about for all to see."

"It's all part of his plan."

"For the record, I'm glad it's Raz and not you."

"I would have done it for Kane."

"I know." That's all I have to say to Kit. It's a thank you. It's respect and appreciation.

He gives me a nod. "Where to next?"

"I want to go visit the team, but I need to take a detour to Mark's place first."

"Why?"

"Because I said," I say, sliding off the barstool to toss the empty box that once held my food that is now in my belly.

It's the only answer I give him and he wouldn't want the truth anyway. I do really want to see if I missed anything, but if Elsa is biting on the taunt me and Ghost have sent her, she's coming to the Hamptons. She might even be here already.

And sometimes the best place to hide is in plain sight, for instance inside her dead brother's house.

CHAPTER THIRTY-TWO

Andrew and my father try to call me on the ride to Mark's house, which can mean nothing good. I don't answer either. Right now, I need to be in my zone, focused, and clearing a path to an end to the killings. Of course, Andrew shoots me a text: *Pocher is trying to send a team of people down here early for the party. We're talking filling up the hotels and restaurants. That's going to create chaos Elsa and Ghost can use to hide.*

My brother is not a dumbass after all. I call him back. "You're right."

"I know I'm right, and I wish like hell I would have thought of this when we first started talking about it. The press is obsessed with him, as is the party, who sees him as a future president."

"I'll kill him before I let that happen and I hope that's recorded. He'll know I mean it. Convince them to stay in the city."

"I tried. That's going to require information you might not want to release and probably your badge and Adams' together."

"I got it." I hang up on him and call my father back.

"Lilah," he greets. "I assume you've heard my security wants the election night events to move to the Hamptons?"

"Yes, and that's not going to happen. There's a hit list. People attending your party are on it."

"Who is on it?"

"Names won't matter if I end this before the party. If you swarm the Hamptons with your people, not only will this person get lost in the crowd, they might just decide to take out a couple extra targets. That doesn't seem like a good way to start your Governorship."

"My team—"

"My badge, and if you want to know how much that means right now, I'm working at the president's discretion."

"*You* are working with the president?" He laughs, the sound pure arrogance. "I find that doubtful."

"Why don't you call him? I'm sure you have a direct line. You are almost the governor."

"I do, actually."

"Good. After you hang up with him, tell the dweeb running your security team, Paul, or whatever his name is, to call me."

"Paul happens to be the best of the best."

I laugh, a real laugh, I have to force myself to stuff. "I don't even want to know what your policy decisions will be if you believe that. He needs to be replaced after election night and I'm only telling you that because Andrew has been roped into working for you and I don't want him to end up dead."

"But it's okay if I get hurt?"

"I guess it would just be the hard lesson you need, Dad, on hiring the wrong people. Kind of like me on the beach that night, right?"

He's silent a beat and then, "Lilah—"

"Don't say anything except, I understand, Agent Mendez."

"I'll handle it," he replies, sounding like he has a stick up his ass and then the line goes dead.

He hung up.

Oh how he must hate having to be submissive to me. There's no way Pocher believes my father won't become power hungry. He has a plan to control him, perhaps some sort of ammunition, on him. I make a mental note to figure out what, later, when I don't have two assassins running around my small town.

I text Andrew: *Call him now. He should do whatever you tell him to do.*

We are talking about the man we call father, right? he replies.

I call him because I don't have a choice. "What happened?" he asks when he answers.

"I told him I'm working for the president."

135

He snorts. "And he believed that?"

"I am working for the president, Andrew. Ellis took me to see him after Murphy was murdered."

"Do I even want to know how that went?"

"He likes to say hogwash. I like to say fuck. It's a relationship destined to fail." Kit pulls up to the Walker house, or as close as he can with the police tape. "I need to go."

"Wait. I think I should go back to the city and make sure we know what Dad's up to."

"Agreed."

"That leaves you with Taylor to contend with."

"If I can't handle a sourpuss chief, I can't handle you and we both know you're my little bitch." I hang up and exit the back door to find Kit already there waiting on me.

"My father's event will remain in the city. I don't want the extra press to scare off my targets, and I damn sure don't want to give Ghost or Elsa extra places to hide." I don't wait for his reply. I head toward the unmanned yellow tape with Kit falling into step with me.

There's one stoney-faced uniform at the door with a bald head and a bit of a belly, with a badge that reads "Berg". Maybe I should invite Berg to the gym with Jay. I cannot stand a cop who doesn't stay fit. It's a sore spot for me. He's risking people's lives. One second too slow and someone dies. Kit's right. The police academy is not the proper place to train Jay. Exactly why I need to start sparring with Kane again. Now. Today.

I flash my badge from where it hangs around my neck. "FBI Special Agent Love," I say, as the name is well known in the town. "Anyone inside right now?"

"No one all day."

"Someone is covering the back door?"

"Yes."

I'd say good, but I'm not sure it matters. The crime scene has been exploited for evidence at this point. "I'm going to take another look inside."

He immediately reaches for his phone.

"What are you doing?" I snap. "Nothing about what I said requires your phone."

"Chief Taylor said to call him if anyone wants in the house."

"Stay with him," I order Kit, "and make sure no one, including Chief Taylor gets in until I say he gets in."

Kit steps forward and takes the phone from the shocked uniform. I open the door and step inside, shutting the door firmly behind me, before I glove up and then lock the door.

But I don't move. There's a slight shift in the air, not even a creak of wood, just a shift. I'm not alone.

CHAPTER THIRTY-THREE

Adrenaline surges through me, the promise of conflict an aphrodisiac to me that most call fear.

I don't pull my weapon. Some would say that's exactly what I should do, but one of the things I did this morning before I ever got in the shower, was sit down and force myself to review my profile of Elsa and write it down this time. In a matter of a few minutes I wrote "she's running on emotions" twenty times.

And "she's alone," another twenty.

I need to know if anyone else is helping her, preparing to take out one or more targets, and I can't find out if she's dead, or in a jail cell with an attorney shutting her up.

There's a blade in my bag that I've been wearing cross-body since before I left the house. With a steady hand I retrieve it and slip it inside my pants pocket.

My speech during the news conference plays in my head, in particular the part where I painted Elsa as a scared loser who practically murdered her own brother. On second thought, I pull my firearm.

Only then do I ease left, and bring the piano into view, careful where my back is at all times.

The body is gone.

The blood tinging the tan carpet beneath black is not.

Mark Walker is now ice cold in a freezer in the morgue which is why there should be a uniform there as well. There better be.

I step further into the room, almost expecting Ghost to be right where he was yesterday, but he's not there. Of course, he's not there. He's smarter than a dumbass and only a dumbass would sit in the open and invite law enforcement to find him.

For a long few moments, I hold my position, listening for another sound, but there's nothing. And yet, there *was* a sound. And there *is* someone here.

I *feel* them.

I ease forward again, and then walk quickly toward the kitchen, inching past the archway to peer inside.

"Lilah."

At the sound of Ghost's voice, I breathe out, relieved when I should not be—he's a killer, a far more lethal one than Elsa, as he's practiced and lacking the weakness of an emotionally driven action.

Ever.

I step fully into the room to find him sitting at the kitchen island, a cup of takeout coffee in front of him, no weapon in sight but there's plenty to see. Holy shit he sounds like Ghost, but he doesn't *look* like Ghost and I remember Kane talking about his chameleon like qualities. "You've changed again."

A smile curves beneath the dark brown of the mustache he's sporting, a really natural looking mustache he didn't have yesterday. "I did, didn't I?" Pride rings in his tone.

He pats the table across from him but I don't move. His cheekbones are higher than before, his brows thicker, his lips fuller. It's makeup, skilled shadowing, a perfect hand, and maybe something more. "It's fucking brilliant."

He laughs, low and deep, and pats the table again and I note how much thicker his neck looks. There's even some girth to his body, at least the part I can see beneath his long sleeved black tee. "Come on," he encourages. "I won't bite. And you don't need the gun."

I believe him. I don't need the gun, not in this moment, but one wrong comment could change that. He's not emotional, but he's so damn cautious, he will never allow himself to be captured. He will never take a risk, not even for an obsession with me.

At this point, I want, no need, to find the real man beneath the disguise so fuck it. I holster my weapon and claim the seat he's suggested, the island separating us, and his green eyes are now brown, his jawline less sharp and square. He must use some sort of putty, a custom made prosthetic perhaps, if that's even possible. Not many people would have the skill to make such a thing, and it's a way to track him down later. Maybe. "Was that you I saw yesterday, the real you?" I ask.

"Do you think I'd let you sketch the real me? You *did* sketch me, didn't you?"

I pull the drawing from my pocket and unfold it, showing it to him. He reaches for it and shows me his hands, confirming he's not holding a weapon on me beneath the table. It's an act of truth. He trusts me. Maybe he is a fool. "Whoever did that is excellent," he concludes and sets it back on the table, as if it's nothing to worry over. "That's badass work."

"You had nothing on your face. That's the real you. It has to be."

He arches one of those extra thick brows. "Was it?"

In other words, I may well have told him my secret, and he showed me absolutely nothing. He's now got leverage over me. He has to know I can't allow that to stand but I won't kill him today, not with an audience outside, and he knows it. Not unless the circumstances were perfect and he will never make the mistake that would require, not with his skill level and experience.

"How long have you been in the house?" I ask.

"I never left."

I'm not really surprised, but I doubt he was in the actual house with the swarm of law enforcement. He was close. He was watching.

"You think she'll come here," I say.

"I think she's coming after you, which is exactly what you wanted. That press conference was money. *You* were brilliant."

"I'm only brilliant if it works."

"It will. We're a good team, me and you, Lilah. I gave her a reason to come. You made sure she found out and you gave her a living reason to come."

"But will she come before she finishes the hits?"

"Yes. She will."

"Why are you so certain?"

"I study my targets. I'm good at knowing what they will do. Just as I knew you'd come back here."

"So I'm a target?"

"No. You are not a target, Lilah."

"But I was yesterday?"

"No." That's all. Nothing more.

My cellphone rings and I pull it from my pocket and he trusts me enough not to even flinch. Or perhaps it's not trust. He's simply arrogant enough to believe his skills superior to mine.

The minute I spy Ellis's number on caller ID I glance at Ghost. "This is my boss who went after Elsa and disappeared. I need to take it."

"Understood," is all he says, his posture unchanging.

I answer the call, and to my shock, I hear, "Agent."

"Ellis?" I ask, shocked to hear his voice.

"Yeah. It's me. She's coming to you and she's losing her mind."

"Elsa?" I ask, my eyes meeting Ghost's stare.

"Yes. I know you know I know her. I tried to convince her to stop this nonsense."

"That was the definition of stupid."

"It distracted her. No one else has died. Not yet. But they will. When I got there she had traps set-up. When she caught me, she tied me up, and proceeded to pace and cry, while I sat there for what felt like eternity. I watched the press conference with her, Agent. It was a brilliant way to flush her out, but she's coming at you hot after leaving me to starve and die. Thankfully Adams came after me" He starts to cough, and not gently.

"Agent."

It's no longer Ellis. "Adams, is he okay?"

"He's pretty beat up. I need to get him to the ER for a checkup and then I'll head your direction, but I have a feeling this is going to blow up before that happens. More soon." He disconnects.

I return my phone to my pocket. "She's coming."

Ghost's mouth curves, but this is not a smile. It's a devious, lethal, satisfied smirk. I'd know that look if I saw it again, no matter what his disguise.

"Killing her saves the rest of your hit list," Ghost states. "You know that, right?"

"I'll handle her. You need to back off."

He pushes to his feet and I follow. He towers over me, a mountain to my hill. Size does matter, and whoever says it doesn't matter, lies. "I'm not going to back off, Agent Mendez," he states. I'm no longer Lilah, signaling the shift between obsession and business. "Now you have a decision to make," he adds. "Are you going to walk out of here and let me do the same?"

I know then that I can't let him leave, but the island is between us, and that makes this about who draws first. And for all I know, he's already drawn beneath the table and his weapon is much bigger than mine, the kind that can blow through the island.

"I won't give you my back," I say.

"Agent Love! Where are you?"

At the sound of Taylor's angry voice, I know Ghost just won. I can stand against Ghost one-on-one and survive, but if Taylor gets in the middle, Taylor is the one who dies.

"Go," I say to Ghost, and a hint of a smile quirks his lips, just a hint. And then he's gone. He doesn't forget his coffee cup that would have held DNA.

And no, his weapon was not drawn.

CHAPTER THIRTY-FOUR

Chief Taylor is angry at the world and he's decided that I'm the world. I exit the kitchen to have him blast me. He literally spews about a hundred words at me, I say absolutely nothing. When he finally takes a breath and settles his hands on his hips, I ask him, "Are you done?"

"Are you?" he snaps back.

"Actually, no." I hold up my badge and say, "I won't be long."

"Did you hear anything I just said to you?"

"No, actually, I didn't. I was thinking about the six people who will be dead soon if I don't catch their future assassin. I'm really good at tuning people out so feel free to follow me around and yell while I work." I start to step around him and pause, "And get someone to check out the attic if you haven't. Now. Not later."

"What the hell is in the attic?"

"That question tells me you haven't checked."

"I didn't run this investigation. I just got here in time for the press conference."

"Then I need to call Andrew and tell him you aren't up to date?"

"What else, Special Agent?" he bites out, knowing full well he should be up to date.

"Expect Elsa to come to the house and the morgue. Be ready for her and unless you want your people to end up dead, I'd consider who they're up against and what she's done. Two highly skilled directors are dead." I step around him and head to the second level, and the master bedroom where I'd found the Ghost's phone number on the pill bottle.

Once I'm in the bedroom, I pull out my phone and lean on the wall, choosing to text my team rather than calling. Not only is the content of my conversations not meant for Taylor, for all I know Ghost has cameras in this place that weren't here yesterday.

I start with Tic Tac: *Check the street cameras around Elsa's place for a tall, dark-haired man with a mustache wearing a blue long sleeved T-shirt. He'll be slightly plump around the middle. If you find him, try to track him to a hotel or residence. And while you're at it, look for Elsa.*

Who is he? he replies.

I'm not about to tell any of them Ghost was here and reap the results that won't be what I want. *The man with one red shoe,* I reply. *Not really. Just find him. Then we'll talk. It's time sensitive.*

I move on to my next text, to Lucas: *Ellis called. Elsa had him tied up. She saw my press conference, and is headed here in an emotional, erratic state. Find her.*

He replies immediately with: *There's a bakery that her and her family went to every holiday. And an inn next door. I'm texting you the address. I'll try to pick her up on the camera feed. More soon. And be careful, cousin. If you die, who will protect me from Kane?*

I don't laugh. I don't answer. Lucas pings the address and I forward it to Kit and say: *Our next stop. I'll be out in ten if Taylor doesn't corner me and next year if he does.*

My last text is to Andrew: *Elsa kidnapped Ellis but he's free and she's on the way to me. Did you check the attic in Mark's house?*

I'm not stupid, Lilah. Of course we did. Nothing but a Christmas tree and a dead mouse. And you need to be careful. I'm serious. Be. Careful.

Yeah, yeah, I think and slide my phone into my pocket. I don't even consider texting Kane about Ghost, not when it changes nothing and hurts his focus. Today is his monthly shareholders update. He can't be distracted and I will not allow all this hell to take what he's worked to build, that has nothing to do with his father's cartel.

I do another quick search of the room in those odd places I often find things—the bottom of the dresser, under the legs of the bed, beneath drawers and so on. I end up back in the bathroom but there's not much to find. As it really should be. Any good forensics team should have gotten anything worth getting. And my brother runs a tight ship.

At this point, I realize I don't know when Elsa would have left Maryland and I have my team randomly searching for her here. I text Adams: *What time does Ellis think Elsa left for New York? And would she fly commercial?*

He answers surprisingly fast: *Hours ago but he's not sure how long and he said no, she won't fly commercial.*

I forward the information to Lucas and have him try to find her point of arrival. In the meantime, hours ago could be longer than Ellis thinks. Elsa could be here and it's time for me to head to her favorite little inn.

CHAPTER THIRTY-FIVE

The ice cream shop and inn are thirty minutes from East Hampton, on Hampton Beach, basically the midway point between North and South Hampton. Somehow it's already lunchtime but speed is critical when it comes to finding Elsa and I ignore my growling belly and head straight to the inn; a cute beachy spot, with the doors open, compliments of a beautiful day, the waves crashing nearby. A massive stone fireplace burns brightly and rather hotly, and there are lots of hotel-ish furnishings and a wood framed front desk.

I greet the attendant, a pretty Asian woman about my age wearing a badge that reads "Vivian" and then slide my FBI identification in front of her.

She glances at it and then me, her eyes brightening with recognition. "I saw you on TV."

"Yes, yes you did. I held a press conference on the Mark Walker murder."

"That's horrible what happened. My boss was telling me that Mark and his family came here every winter for a decade."

Bingo. Maybe? "Have they been in recently?"

"No. In fact Anna, that's my boss, said she was shocked to hear Mark lived here."

No bingo on this card. "I'm looking for his sister. We're worried about her. She's lost Mark, and both of her parent's fairly recently."

"Oh my. How tragic. I don't remember her by name."

I pull up the photo of Elsa on my phone and slide it in front of Vivian. "This is her."

"Hmmmm. She's pretty. That red hair is glorious. I'd remember her." She shakes her head. "She hasn't been in, not when I was on duty which has been often." She keys into her computer. "Let me check our recent check-ins."

We talk through her list, and it's a dead end, it seems. "She might not have red hair right now," I push gently.

"I still think I'd recognize her. I'd certainly know the name."

"Is Anna here? Maybe she can help?"

"No. She actually left for vacation a few days ago. Her mom's in a nursing home in Westbury and she's moving her to a place a little closer. I guess that doesn't seem like much of a vacation." She waves away the comment with her hand. "She called me to check in and that is when she told me about Mark."

"That makes sense." I pass my card to her. "Can you have her call me? And can you call me if you see Elsa?"

"Yes. I'd be happy to."

"Just don't tell her you recognize her or that you're calling me. We're very concerned she might need some sort of help and I don't want to spook her."

She lowers her voice conspiratorially. "Is someone trying to kill her, too?"

"It's better safe than sorry."

We chat a bit more and when I depart, I'm feeling good about her calling me should she see Elsa, but Elsa knows we are looking for her. She'll alter her appearance, not as well as Ghost, but she'll make changes.

I exit the front door as Kit pushes off the wall and falls into step with me. Clearly he's the only person Kane trusts with me up against Ghost, as I suggested yet again that Jay trade places with him and got declined.

"What's next?" he asks.

"Food. Let's hit the sandwich joint across from the ice cream shop, and we can just hang out a bit and see if she materializes. If not, we'll divide up and hit the cluster of shopping surrounding us and show her photo to people.

A few minutes later, Kit has a giant meatball sub and I have Avocado toast which is extra healthy because I'm not saying no to ice cream. And I like Avocado toast. It's a win, win. We eat in silence, both intensely studying our surroundings, the lack of words a non-issue. We talked on the ride to the beach when I asked him if he too had seen the brutality of Kane's father and he said simply, "Yes," and offered nothing more.

Kit and Jay are night and day. Jay spits out words like he's handing out money everyone wants. Kit chokes on the very idea of the very same words.

We finish eating, sit a while, and when I would leave our table behind and head across the way to the ice cream shop, Kit objects. "You pissed her off. She's emotional. She's a sniper. Going to Elsa's favorite ice cream shop might send her over the edge. I'll get you ice cream."

I hate that he's right. "Fine. I'll look at the flavors online real quick. And I want hot fudge no matter what." After a quick scan I pick pistachio peach and pistachio chocolate.

Kit exits the restaurant and I watch him enter the ice cream shop, keeping my attention keenly aware. A woman with dark hair draping her face walks out of the ice cream shop that I don't remember seeing go in, but it might have been when I was distracted by Kit leaving the sandwich joint.

The woman sits at a table with her back to me, enjoying the warmer weather, and then to my shock immediately after, Kit exits, no ice cream in hand, and to my surprise he sits down with the woman.

Elsa.

It has to be Elsa.

I push to my feet, and head for the door, thankful for the flats I keep in my bag and changed into on the way over here. My hand slips under my jack and settles on my weapon. I exit the restaurant and find Kit walking toward me. The woman remains at her table and makes no effort to run or escape.

"She's an old friend of Elsa's," he explains. "Nothing overly helpful. Let's go inside. I don't want you in the open."

Disappointment stabs at me, but the ice cream in my future helps. We have to take a number and wait our turn. We sit at a corner table, out of the earshot of the rest of the visitors. "I heard Luna," Kit explains, "that's the woman I sat down with, talking to the owner of the shop about Elsa. The owner doesn't know her, but Luna told her all about going to school with her."

"And?

"She hasn't seen her in years. I don't think Elsa would risk coming to a place where everyone knows her."

It's not an unfamiliar thought. I've had it myself and I agree with it, at least for the most part—but—and it's a big but—Elsa also just lost her brother. Comfort is a human need and the familiar filled with memories can be just that. No sooner do I have the thought, than a woman walks in the door, a beanie covering her hair with what I think is a bad black wig underneath.

Her eyes rocket to mine and I know without question this is Elsa. As if proving my point, she turns and exits the ice cream shop. I'm on my feet and behind her in a blink, and with luck on my side, an old lady trips up Elsa. My luck ends when Elsa grabs the yelping woman and turns her toward me.

I grab her arms to move her but the woman yells out, "Help!" and then smashes her ice cream sundae, a rather big one, in my face. Cold sticky sundae mess consumes me and I'm blinded by hot fudge and whipped cream and it's my turn to turn with the woman to get her out of my path.

Kit curses as I plant her against him, and then grab a stack of napkins, as I run fairly blindly, toward a cluster of shops, a worthless endeavor. Elsa is gone and I halt, aware that most of these shores will have a backdoor for parking and trash. I dial Tic Tac who answers on the first ring. "Any news?" he asks.

"We found her and lost her. Have Chief Taylor get a team canvassing the area though I don't think they'll find her. We won't see her again until she wants us, too. And give Taylor my number and tell him to text me his. I'm going home to change and then coming to you next."

"Change why?"

"I got a little ice cream all over me." I don't elaborate. I disconnect.

At this point, Kit is by my side, and he gives a grunt. "That went like shit. We looked like fools on some sort of hidden camera show."

He's not wrong and I lick chocolate from my lip. "The hot fudge is damn good. We owe the old lady ice cream for life. Let's go make that happen and get some for us for the road."

"I'm not going to argue. I either need a shot or ice cream. Hanging out with you is stressful as fuck, Lilah."

"Oh stop being a whiny baby. You're getting ice cream."

This is over. At least, for now.

Not much later the old lady has her ice cream for a year for free, and the security guard has a pint to take home. But as I enjoy my pistachio with immense pleasure, Kit's words play in my head. *Going to Elsa's favorite ice cream shop might send her over the edge.* I mean maybe. I could get very personal and protective over this ice cream.

CHAPTER THIRTY-SIX

"Everyone here needs to take a shower!"

I walk into Lucas's place and its rank. After a quick inspection I find them all in the combination living room and kitchen; Enrique and Jay watching TV while Lucas and Tic Tac sit across from each other at the kitchen table with laptops in front of them and Jack at the endcap. There's also an open container of sushi in front of Lucas.

"You know you smell like that stuff after you eat?" I demand, grabbing it and taking it to the trash where I dump it, in a scent-controlling sealed can.

"Damn it, I was eating that, Lilah," Lucas whines.

"We agree with Lilah," Jay calls out. "Which is why we ordered pizza."

"Jack solved the waitress mystery," Tic Tac says, strangely silent on the sushi, which means he's a second offender. This is why I don't like to be around people. I find out the gross things they do.

Kit joins his men and I sit down on the opposite endcap to Jack. "I'm listening."

"I went into the diner today and flirted with one of the waitresses."

The idea of him doing any such thing is downright comical. "You. Flirted? Did you describe the way Michael killed victim number three in *Halloween 2*?"

"No. Should I have? I remember exactly. It was a dark night and—"

"No. Please. I beg of you, do not tell me. Just get to the part where you solved the mystery."

"Marissa, that's the waitress I just met, she told me they were all paid to know nothing. And what do they know?"

"She doesn't know. She wasn't a part of it, but she says that Meghan who works tonight got paid. And she's real nervous. If you ask her with your badge as decoration, she says Meghan will talk."

I'm skeptical but Murphy left me that card to the diner, this new information suggests a large, payday-worthy secret. "When does she get in?"

"Seven."

"Then we'll go to dinner at seven." I conclude.

"We, including me," Kit calls out.

"Only if you stay out of sight, and in the parking lot," I say. "I need Elsa to get bold and come at me so she doesn't shift back to her target list. And before you argue," I rotate to face him, "I'm an FBI agent. I do shit like this and if you don't like it, I'll arrest you and if you don't believe me, try me."

"Kane won't like it."

"Kane has a love-hate relationship with my badge, and if he wants the part he loves, he needs to deal with the part he hates. And yes, I'll say that to him, but he's a little busy right now." I turn back around and offer my attention to Tic Tac and Lucas. "What else do we have?"

"I got my hands on Elsa's discharge file," Lucas offers. "She was forced out on a mental health recommendation, but from what I can tell, she was fine after her exit. She opened her business. She goes to the gym. She actually does charity work for wounded warriors."

My brows dip as I try to work through this. "Then what set her off now? Why create a hit list and act on it now?"

"I can answer that," Tic Tac offers. "The government had been trying to buy her father's property for years, for big money, too. She said no. And when they finally used a law, I'll spare you the details on, to force her to sell, she was not happy. Neither was Mark. He got some big named attorneys involved. It's tied up in the legal system now, but it's not looking good for Elsa and Mark."

"Okay, then. Good work, everyone. I don't think Elsa is coming for any of you, but coming at you would be coming at me, so stick together to be safe." I push to my feet. "I'm going home to get some quality time in Purgatory. I need to think."

"What's bothering you?" Jack asks.

"Her. And how she got here."

"You want me to come with you?" Jack asks. "We can go straight from there to the diner."

"No, Jack. I do not want you to come with me. Jay can bring you to the diner." I step back into the living room. "Oh and Jay, I got you out of the police academy. Kit is going to get someone he knows to train you."

Kit's lips twitch ever so slightly. He's obviously aware that I'm just giving Jay a hard time but also a wake-up call. Something has to change.

Jay pales, white as a winter's day. "Raz? Isn't he replacing the kingpin?"

"Yes," I confirm, "and I never said it was Raz, but if you survive whoever it is, you can survive anything. We'll get you started right after the election."

"I'll train him," Enrique says. "I know what needs to change."

I consider him a moment, aware of the darkness beneath his surface that's balanced with loyalty. "If Raz isn't available for some reason, like his new job calls him in, Enrique gets the job." I head for the door, and Kit follows, my shadow, but I have a feeling he's not my only shadow.

And that's why I agree to go to dinner with Jack. It's not about Jack. It's about letting Elsa find me.

CHAPTER THIRTY-SEVEN

Purgatory turns into phone calls.

I'm on the floor with my jacket and shoes off, and notecards in front of me, just to make sure I have my head on straight for this case, when Adams calls. "Ellis is in the hospital. Apparently, she saw his role on the committee that took that contract from Clyde as the biggest betrayal of all. She was going to kill him, but a bullet was good enough. She wanted him to beg for his life."

"How bad is he?"

"He had to have surgery on his arm, a pin in the wrist. He's stable and stubborn enough to insist he be flown there tomorrow. He feels he can distract her from the other targets. He even wants to do a press conference."

Ellis just earned a little respect from me. A little. We'll see where that leads. "When are you coming back?"

"Tonight. I have depositions in the morning. Fucking Murphy was so obsessed with one target that he did some shitty things to end other cases."

I notice how he doesn't say "Society" over the phone line. He clearly knows the Society was all Murphy lived for, but just how much he knows is for later. "Oh and Ellis told me to tell you, everything he discussed with you still stands."

In other words, Ellis still wants me to work for him and spy on Adams. And yet he trusted Adams to save his life? I'm going to need a lot of answers to work for any of these people.

My next few hours involve ME's, the NYC chief of the police department who still wanted to know about Murphy since his murder happened on his territory, and my brother. "So she's really here," he says after I rundown what happened today.

"She is. How ready are you for her?"

"As ready as we can be. Why don't we tell the targets to stay home?"

"If we do that, Elsa may go underground indefinitely and considering I've pissed her off, I need this to be her or me, sooner than later."

We've just hung up when Kane calls. "I heard you were attacked by ice cream."

"An ice cream sundae to be precise and it was excellent. When this is over we have to go to that ice cream shop."

"She got too close to you, Lilah."

"I got close to her. She had no idea I was there. And I'm going to the diner tonight with Jack to try to talk to some waitress who might know something about the mysterious other waitress. Kit and team need to stay outside." I don't wait for an answer. "When are you coming home?"

"It'll be late. When I got out of my meetings, I had ten million dollar oil well start spilling. Be careful tonight."

"I'm always careful."

"You're never careful."

"No. I'll start tomorrow."

He lowers his voice and says something dirty to me in Spanish followed by something wildly romantic and then he's gone. I start scribbling on my notecards. *Be careful,* I write.

Where was Ghost today?

I led him right to Elsa today.

But he did nothing.

Unless...she's already dead?

No. He'd call me and brag.

My gut says Elsa and Ghost are both alive and following me and that can end only one way, and that's bloody. Tonight could be just another night Jack jabbers about horror movies while I don't listen. Or...not.

CHAPTER THIRTY-EIGHT

Jack meets me at the diner by my design.

Less time to talk. And talk. And talk.

At present we're sitting at the far table near the bathrooms, which is always the best seat in the house, waiting for Marissa to get in. She's late but this is her table when she finally arrives. In the meantime, I drink coffee, or rather spoon it, as it's covered in whipped cream, and Jack, well, he's Jack and he's making up for lost time in the talking category.

"Did you know that one of the *Candyman* killings was based on a true Chicago crime story? And the bees were real. Plus—"

"Is that her?" I ask, as I have eyes on the front door and he does not.

He twists around and then faces me again. "That's her. She's pretty, right? Kind of Barbie-like? She'd be the first one to die in a *Friday the 13th* movie and that's a real compliment. Shit. Maybe I shouldn't have ordered that steak. I'll look gluttonous right?"

It's only now that I realize his hair is slicked back and his collar shirt well pressed. Pressed. He has a crush. Thankfully not on me. "I told you not to order the steak," I chide. "I really don't want to see you chewing on meat."

He pales. "What? Why? Do I chew meat funny? Have you ever seen me chew meat?"

Marissa appears at our table and sets his steak in front of him and I guess her to be in her mid-twenties and he's right. She's pretty in a doll-like way. "Hi Jack," she greets, and pulls a bottle of steak sauce and a knife from her apron and sets them beside him. "Good to see you. I ah—"

"Hi," Jack says, sounding as nervous as he looks, his voice quaking.

"I'm glad you came back in." I shift slightly and her gaze rockets to me. "Oh. I'm sorry. Let me get your cake." She rushes away.

Jack gives me an incredulous look. "You got cake. What happened to the pie?"

"I want cake," is all I say, but what I don't say is that if Ghost is watching, I want him to know he ruined my pie for me. At least right now.

"Should I eat the steak in front of her?" he asks, and grabs his fork and knife and starts cutting.

"If you want to be chewing while she's talking to you."

"I can't just stare at it." He stuffs a bite in his mouth and starts chewing. And chewing.

"They're tough as rubber here," I say. "That's why I said, don't get the steak."

Marissa returns and sets my Italian cream cake in front of me. It looks delicious and not at all healthy. I'll try again tomorrow. I lift my badge and show it to Marissa. "FBI."

Her gaze rockets to Jack who's still chewing. "You set me up."

He shakes his head. "No." He grabs a napkin and spits out the steak. "No. It's just—"

"Tell me about the waitress that went to Nashville. Or do I need to talk to Meghan. Where is she?"

She purses her lips and squats. "That was me. I just said Meghan. I was nervous. Jill Havens is her name. She had an affair with that man who was murdered. The wife found out and threatened her and she was very upset. The word is Mark sent her to Italy, not Nashville, where her sister is working, to get her away from his wife, but they divorced anyway."

"Why is everyone so secretive?"

"The wife threatened some people here. Or ex-wife now. They feel like she will be spiteful to Jill or us for hiding her. The owner was really scared. She told us to be quiet. And I'm not feeling well tonight. I thought it was over but it's not. I need to go to the bathroom."

The minute she walks away, I text Tic Tac everything and get him investigating it. "Did I just win a spot on the team?" Jack asks, beaming now and shoving aside his rubber steak.

"Right now, all I can see is you chewing that steak so ask me later."

"That's not a no."

My phone rings with Tic Tac's number and I answer. "What's up?"

"Mark went to Italy last month. He made transfers to an account in Italy as well. Lucas is tracing it. Wait." Lucas says something to him. "He already got it. Jill Havens." Lucas murmurs something else and then Tic Tac adds, "We have her address she shares with Melissa Havens and both work at a fashion designer."

"Okay, then. I guess Murphy was just making the connection to Mark. Maybe for his own purposes, not mine, but at least we know."

I sigh. "So not much of a lead, just soap opera material."

"Afraid so," Tic Tac replies.

And when we hang up, Jack is waiting, fork in hand. "Can I try your cake?"

"I haven't even tried my cake, so no you cannot try my cake."

Someone sets a pie on the table in between us, one of the other waitresses. "Someone called and asked us to give this to you. Said to tell you it's from a secret admirer. It's a lot of pie. We can box what you don't eat."

Ghost.

He's telling me he's not only here, he knows I didn't order the pie. He must have cameras in here.

"This is amazing," Jack declares. "I've always wanted to try the famous pie." He grabs his steak knife. "May I?"

"Don't use your steak knife, Jack. Use a regular knife."

"Right. Right." He grabs one and when he would cut the pie, he suddenly starts screaming, and I mean screaming like a little kid who's sibling just hit him.

I have a moment of thinking he's a fool, but he's pointing to my left and my gaze jerks to the woman wearing an ill fitted uniform standing next to me holding a gun.

Elsa.

Instinct kicks in and I reach for the knife at the same time Jack grabs the pie and shoves it in Elsa's face. In that moment, she stumbles and the gun cracks against the ground as it hits hard but thankfully does not go off. I'm on foot, prepared to engage, and she reaches for my weapon. Somehow that steak knife is in my hand and I drive it as hard as I can at her. We both slip on the damn pie and it lands in her arm which isn't going to do the right kind of damage to stop her attack.

But Elsa whales in pain, and right when I would go in for another attack, Jack slams into me and the next thing I know I'm on the ground, with him on top of me. "Are you crazy?! Get up. Get off. What are you doing?"

"I was trying to tackle her but I slipped."

I shove him off or me or he half rolls, I don't know, but I'm furious. By the time I'm on my feet again. Elsa is gone and people are screaming, "Back door! Back door, Agent Love!"

I race into the hallway, and open the exit door to find Elsa lying on the ground. She's dead and I don't have to ask by what method. I know a broken neck when I see one. It's Ghost. He did this.

My phone buzzes with a text message and I already know it's from him before I pull my phone out and read: *I'm number one again. You know what that means. And don't forget the pie.*

CHAPTER THIRTY-NINE

Hours later, after way too much Chief Taylor for my sanity, and ten thousand apologies from Jack, I'm done for the night. Kane picks me up in one of his fancy sports cars and we end up at the kitchen island, eating pizza again, because there's nothing else this time of night.

But Kane can't stop laughing long enough to eat. "Elsa smashed ice cream in your face. Then Jack shoved a pie in her face and tackled you."

"How many times are you going to repeat that?" I shove pizza in my mouth.

"There's not many things that make me laugh like this, bella, but it sounds like a bad comedy."

"Yeah, well, Jack and his pie probably saved my life yet again."

"Hire him, Lilah. He deserves it."

"He spit meat in his napkin."

His brows inch up. "I don't even want to know what that means."

"Exactly. But okay, yes. I'll hire him. You think Ghost is going to go after my father?"

"Do you?"

"I think he will. I think it's going to be at the party."

"Me too, bella. And we'll be ready."

"I question the validity of that statement so I'm just going to point out a positive about tonight."

"You lived?"

"And I didn't stab her to death. I didn't arrest her, but I wasn't the one who killed Elsa."

"That's a good thing, but feel free to stab Ghost as many times and ways as you wish. Do not hesitate, Lilah, or you will be dead."

CHAPTER FORTY

The few days leading up to election night are a rush of paperwork and activity that lands us in New York City a day early. Andrew is at the airport when we arrive, eager to talk in person and he doesn't even care that Kane is with me. We're still in the airport when he breaches the obvious topic, "Are we going to let him kill Dad?"

"Do you still have the elevated security for tomorrow night?"

"Yes."

"Then he's protected."

He narrows eyes on me. "You think he's coming for him."

"Ghost does the unexpected."

"Should we warn Dad?"

"We'll be there, Andrew. Kane has men with him at all times, and he also has his secret service. That's a hard number to crack even for Ghost."

"Right."

I don't ask what he wants to happen. He's conflicted. I get that, but I'm not as conflicted as he is. Every time I think about him like a real father, I remember that beach, that man. The way he felt on top of me.

After we part with Andrew, we head home but stop by the hospital to see Ellis, who's about to have a second surgery on his arm. Kane hangs out at the coffee shop while I visit with the man who wants to be my boss. He's a mess with pins in his arms and his face is puffy, no doubt from all the fluid they're pumping in him.

"You got beat up by a woman and want me to work for you?" I tease softly, sitting next to him, my arms on the steel railings.

"I do."

"You seem to trust Adams."

"I don't."

I grimace. "Why?"

"Not here. Just keep an open mind and be careful tomorrow night. You'll be in the hive."

Of the Society, he means.

And my brother is living in the hive.

I'm not scared for my father, but I am for Andrew, and not because of Ghost.

CHAPTER FORTY-ONE

Of course, my father has demanded me and Kane attend a number of pre-functions for his election night, but thanks to Elsa I have an excuse the public will understand for not being present.

But election night is another story.

I dress in a red dress and Kane matches me in a red tie. When I should be putting final touches on my makeup, I find myself standing at our bedroom window, staring out at the Manhattan skyline, lights twinkling, stars dancing. Kane steps to my side. "What's on your mind? Ghost?"

"This." I hand him the baggie in my hand, the earring and note Jay had found at Murphy's place inside.

"1900. You know where," he reads, his brow furrowed. "What is this?"

"I can't believe I haven't shown it to you before now. Jay found it in Murphy's coat in the closet. That's my mother's earring."

"Does it mean anything to you?"

"No. Tic Tac tried to find some sort of link to that number and failed. He just texted me. Elsa had consumed him but now that he's free...he tried."

"He's very loyal to you."

"He is. He really tried. The number must be a time, but I wonder if I'll ever know all there was to know about that message, and so many things to do with my mother."

Kane sets the baggie on the window ledge, and catches my shoulders, turning me to face him. "We will find the answers you need to find peace, Lilah. I will do anything to make it so."

My heart squeezes and I push to my toes and kiss him. "I know or you would not be going to this event tonight."

***

Not much later, we're in a limo my father sent for us when Kane receives a text and I know immediately from the tension rippling through his body, something's wrong.

I touch his arm and he leans in close and whispers, "The mob's best assassin is missing, as is my father."

I jerk back to look at him. "You have got to be fucking kidding."

"I wish I was."

It feels like an omen for the night.

And true to that, not long later, we find ourselves standing among my father's supporters, with poll numbers whispered to us constantly. It's not even a race and my father will be the next Governor. It's a long tedious night but Kane and I decided we'd use this time to meet those close to my father, in the "hive" and find every useful nugget of information we can while here.

The race is close to being called and the crowd is rowdy with excitement. I'm shoved into Kane, even as he continues to talk to some door, and I feel someone shove something in the pocket of my dress. Disturbed and worried it's Ghost, I retrieve what is a white piece of paper and read: *Red, white and blue, the land of lies. But SHE has the truth.*

Junior, my long last, note writer, why are you back now? And at least your poem isn't as ridiculous as some of them have been. I shove it back in my pocket and Andrew catches my arm. "We're about to announce but he wants to see you before he goes on stage."

Whatever, I think, but I push to my toes and tell Kane before I follow Andrew. We end up backstage, where there's a door that I assume is my father's dressing room. "He said just go in."

"Where are you going?"

"I need to make sure the press is in position."

"Liar. You just want to throw me to the wolves." But he's already walking away.

I open the door and step inside, but have to pull back a curtain to truly enter the room. That's when I stop dead in my tracks. My father is sitting in a chair with Ghost holding a gun to his head, this time with a full brown beard but the extra weight is gone.

Adrenaline surges but I feel no fear. "Ghost. What are you doing?"

"You know him?" my father snaps. "What the fuck, Lilah?"

Ghost ignores him. "I told you I'd do this for you, Lilah," he says. "I owe you."

"Do what?" my father demands.

"I didn't ask you to do this," I say, and because I want my father to feel the pain of this, I add, "I didn't ask you to kill him."

"Kill me?! What the hell?!"

Ghost yanks his hair back and says, "Scream and I stop asking Lilah what she wants and end you. You sent someone to rape and kill her."

"That's not what happened," my father objects. "I didn't do it."

Ghosts squats to his ear level and growls. "Then who did?"

"I can't tell you."

Because it was him. And Pocher. I hate him, but I still say, "This is unlike you, Ghost. You can't get away with this here."

"You still underestimate me. Why?"

"Don't do this." My voice is steady. I'm steady.

He narrows eyes on me, *blue eyes*, I believe this time. "Ever? Or now?"

I consider that a moment and let the truth, my truth, form my response. "He's mine. When the time is right, he's mine."

Ghost studies me, really looks at me, and says, "You have a reason to keep him alive now." It's not a question.

To take down the Society, I think, but I don't speak it. I simply say, "Yes."

"All right then. He needs to know that if he touches you again, if he speaks against you about this tonight, he'll meet me again. And he won't live to meet me a third time. He needs to know some of the pain he caused you or I can't walk out of here."

He waits, as if waiting for my approval. "Okay."

"Leave the room."

"He has to go on camera in a few minutes."

"He will."

"I'm staying."

He shrugs and before I know his intent, he grabs my father's hand and then leans to his ear again, whispers something I don't understand before speaking to me again. "Until next time, Lilah." He breaks my father's finger and then just like that, he's out a back exit, and if I'm right, he won't look like the same person he does now when he leaves.

My father doesn't scream as if Ghost has forbidden it. He cries, like a baby.

And just like that, Ghost is gone.

And Junior is back.

The End...for now

THE LILAH LOVE SERIES CONTINUES IN *JUNIOR HAS A SECRET* WHICH IS AVAILABLE FOR PRE-ORDER NOW!

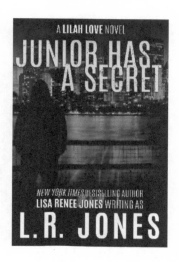

HTTPS://WWW.LISARENEEJONESTHRILLERS.COM/THE-LILAH-LOVE-SERIES.HTML#JUNIOR

***

GET THE FIRST LOOK AT MY NEW THRILLER:

YOU LOOK BEAUTIFUL TONIGHT

Mia Anderson is an invisible woman. An unremarkable thirty-two-year-old Tennessee librarian, she's accustomed to disappearing in a crowd, unseen and unheard. Then she receives an anonymous note: You look beautiful tonight . . .

It doesn't stop there. The attentive stranger—a secret admirer named Adam—has plans for Mia. With each new text comes Adam's suggestions for hair, clothes, and attitude. For the first time in memory, Mia feels noticed. Slowly, Mia develops a confidence in herself she's never had. But Adam has a surprise coming...Mia finally sees Adam for who he is, and what he's prepared to do for her. Even kill.

Fearing she could be implicated in the murder, Mia's forced to turn to the stranger in the shadows watching her every move. Adam's game of cat and mouse begins. Mia is the prey. In order to survive, she must also become the predator.

LEARN MORE:

HTTPS://WWW.LISARENEEJONESTHRILLERS.COM/YOU-LOOK-BEAUTIFUL-TONIGHT.HTML

***

GET A PERFECT LIE TODAY!

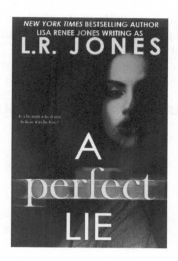

I'm Hailey Anne Monroe. I'm twenty-eight years old. An artist, who found her muse on the canvas because I wasn't allowed to have friends or even keep a journal. And yes, if you haven't guessed by now, I'm that Hailey Anne Monroe, daughter to Thomas Frank Monroe, the man who was a half-percentage point from becoming President of the United States. If you were able to ask him, he'd probably tell you that I was the half point. But you can't ask him, and he can't tell you. He's dead. They're all dead and now I can speak.

LEARN MORE:

HTTPS://WWW.LISARENEEJONESTHRILLERS.COM/A-PERFECT-LIE.HTML

***

BE THE FIRST TO KNOW!
The best way to be informed of all upcoming books, sales, giveaways, television news (there's some coming soon!), and to get a FREE EBOOK, be sure you're signed up for my newsletter list!

SIGN-UP HERE:
HTTP://LISARENEEJONES.COM/NEWSLETTER-SIGN-UP/

ALSO BY LISA RENEE JONES

THE INSIDE OUT SERIES
If I Were You
Being Me
Revealing Us
His Secrets*
Rebecca's Lost Journals
The Master Undone*
My Hunger*
No In Between
My Control*
I Belong to You
All of Me*

THE SECRET LIFE OF AMY BENSEN
Escaping Reality
Infinite Possibilities
Forsaken
Unbroken*

CARELESS WHISPERS
Denial
Demand
Surrender

WHITE LIES
Provocative
Shameless

TALL, DARK & DEADLY / WALKER SECURITY
Hot Secrets

Dangerous Secrets
Beneath the Secrets
Deep Under
Pulled Under
Falling Under
Savage Hunger
Savage Burn
Savage Love
Savage Ending
When He's Dirty
When He's Bad
When He's Wild
Luke's Sin
Luke's Touch
Luke's Revenge
Adam's Temptation (2025)

LILAH LOVE
Murder Notes
Murder Girl
Love Me Dead
Love Kills
Bloody Vows
Bloody Love
Happy Death Day
The Party Is Over
The Ghost Assassin
Agent vs. Assassin
Junior Has a Secret (2025)

DALTON FAMILY TRILOGY
My Enemy, My Obsession
The Bargain

SCANDALOUS BILLIONAIRES
Beautiful Betrayal
Filthy Deal

Naked Truth
Dirty Lawyer
Dirty Boss
Dirty Rival
Wicked Secrets
Wicked Submission

WINDWALKERS

He is Creed Part One
He is Creed Part Two
He is Creed Part Three
He is Jensen Part One
He is Jensen Part Two

DIRTY RICH

Dirty Rich One Night Stand
Dirty Rich Cinderella Story
Dirty Rich Obsession
Dirty Rich Betrayal
Dirty Rich Cinderella Story: Ever After
Dirty Rich One Night Stand: Two Years Later
Dirty Rich Obsession: All Mine
Dirty Rich Secrets
Dirty Rich Betrayal: Love Me Forever
His Demand
Her Submission

THE FILTHY TRILOGY

The Bastard
The Princess
The Empire

THE NAKED TRILOGY

One Man
One Woman
Two Together

THE BRILLIANCE TRILOGY
A Reckless Note
A Wicked Song
A Sinful Encore

THE NECKLACE TRILOGY
What If I Never
Because I Can
When I Say Yes

THE TYLER & BELLA TRILOGY
Bastard Boss
Sweet Sinner
Dirty Little Vow

WALL STREET EMPIRE
Protégé King
Scorned Queen
Burned Dynasty

STANDALONE THRILLERS
You Look Beautiful Tonight
The Wedding Party
A Perfect Lie
The Poet

*eBook only

ABOUT LISA RENEE JONES

New York Times and *USA Today* bestselling author Lisa Renee Jones writes dark, edgy fiction including the highly acclaimed *Inside Out* series and the crime thriller *The Poet*. Suzanne Todd (producer of Alice in Wonderland and Bad Moms) on the *Inside Out* series: *Lisa has created a beautiful, complicated, and sensual world that is filled with intrigue and suspense.*

Prior to publishing, Lisa owned a multi-state staffing agency that was recognized many times by The Austin Business Journal and also praised by the Dallas Women's Magazine. In 1998 Lisa was listed as the #7 growing women-owned business in Entrepreneur Magazine. She lives in Colorado with her husband, a cat that talks too much, and a Golden Retriever who is afraid of trash bags.

Made in United States
Troutdale, OR
01/10/2025

27807926R00108